The Cave Journals
A Detective Joe Craig Novel

by Dennis Ray

This book is a work of the authors imagination. Names, characters, and places are my imagination at work. When a real name or place is used, it is used fictitiously. This book may not be reproduced, transmitted electronically, or photo copied without the express written permission of the author or publisher, except where permitted by law.

DEDICATION

This book is dedicated to my sister Pam for all of her patience with me and for her countless hours of decoding my writings as she edited this book. I will be forever grateful.

And to my wife Willie as she worked hard so I could sit back in my easy chair and write this story

THE CAVE JOURNALS
PART ONE

CHAPTER ONE

I'm about to tell you a story that I have kept a secret for fifty years. My name is Joe Craig, and I am a private detective living in Plymouth, Indiana, a small town of a few thousand at the time of this story.

I was 30 years old then with many cases under my belt. My friends called me Shutdown Joe because I had either finished or solved every case I was on—must have been that German ingenuity and affinity for details that my ancestors brought with them in the 1920's when they left the old country for a better life. At 6 foot 4 and 180 pounds, Clint Eastwood could have been my twin. I was single and liked it that way. I had no pets, as I was usually not home long enough to take care of them. I usually took on small cases—cheating husbands and wives, lost jewelry, and the like; but on occasion, I took a big case when I felt the need for a challenge. I had just finished a job where a high-ranking official embezzled money from the government. I was paid well for that job, and I immediately went out and bought my dream car, a navy blue 1967 Camaro SS with a 350 under the hood and four-on-the-floor. Life couldn't get much better it seemed, but that was about to change. And I mean change.

It was the summer of 1967. The year my life changed forever.

I had just finished washing my Camaro when my neighbor, Mrs. Cryer called to me from her porch.

"Joe! Joe, when you have time can you come over? I need to talk to you. It's very important!" Mrs. Cryer was a friendly old lady. She would often call me over for a glass of lemonade and tell me what had gone on in the neighborhood while I was gone. Her husband had just died and she was lonely. I went over expecting to once again just sit on the porch, but she asked me to come in. I had never been in her house and was surprised to see that it was a modest home—not shabby, not fancy. Family pictures on the walls and a fireplace mantel covered with dusty trinkets told me there were many memories here. She asked me to come into the kitchen and have a glass of lemonade while she talked.

"Joe, I want to tell you a story. At the beginning of the year, my husband Bill was put in jail for being drunk and rowdy at the Blue Bar down in Logansport. He was transferred to the Plymouth jail because there was a warrant out for him for punching a man in the face.

"One weekend, an old man came into the jail. He said his sentence was to spend every Saturday and Sunday there for a month, and that his job was to do whatever the sheriff needed done. Well, that Sunday morning, the sheriff had the old man clean the jailhouse basement. Bill said the strangest thing happened.

"'Bill, look down here!' The old man yelled. My husband looked down at the floor, and in the corner was a hole—a perfectly round hole. There was also the same kind of hole in the ceiling, like an old stovepipe used to be there. Anyway, my husband got on the floor and looked through the hole and saw the old man in the basement. He then told Bill to put his hand in the hole. Bill did. The old man stuck a warm beer in his hand. He then hollered for Bill to take another. You can imagine Bill's surprise at getting served beer in jail. A few minutes later, the old man came back upstairs and went to my husband's cell. He introduced himself as Mark Binger, grabbed one of the warm cans of beer, opened it, and said, 'Cheers.' Bill did the same.

"They chatted for a while until the sheriff told Mark to take out the trash before he left; we were to crush our cans very small so no one could see that we had been drinking beer. The sheriff told the old man he could leave early. Mark said goodbye to Bill and left. Bill said that when he started to get off his bed, a wet piece of paper floated to the floor from his lap. He picked it up. It was a business card with the wet impression of the bottom of the beer can.

"Joe," Mrs. Cryer said in a low voice, "it was a business card from the Blue Bar in Logansport. The back of it said, 'Bill, be sure the latest shipment makes it to the house on the hill.'

"My husband was released from jail the next day, and a court date was set; but shortly after he got home and told me what had happened, he had a fatal heart attack. As I held him, he whispered to me that there was a satchel hidden in a closet at a house on Erie Ave. in Logansport that would lead me to a treasure—enough money to last me the rest of my life. Then he died. Joe, I don't know what treasure he was talking about. And I know I'm being watched. Everywhere I go, I feel someone is watching me. Who knew my husband was in the Plymouth jail to leave him that card? And why did my husband have a heart attack so soon after? Why did..."

"Whoa, whoa now, Mrs. Cryer, I said. " That's quite a story. Let me do a little digging and I'll get back to you."

Mrs. Cryer continued as if she hadn't heard me.

"I went through his desk and couldn't find any mention of a treasure, but I did find a hand-drawn street map." Mrs. Cryer walked to the desk and brought back a folded paper. "See here, Joe? It looks like a cemetery across from a row of houses. One of them has a big X over it."

I took the map and told her I would get on it first thing in the morning. What the heck, I had a few days with nothing lined up, so why not?

I went back home and did a few chores. I swept the kitchen floor, did a little mopping, and wondered if I needed to get a pet cat or dog. No, too much work. Maybe a turtle? Then I laughed at myself and decided I should go grab a quick bite.

It was about 6 p.m., so I drove my new Camaro over

to Adams Street where there was a nice little corner cafe. Nan, a hard-working waitress who was still in high school and looked like a young Marilyn Monroe, took my order.

"Just a cheeseburger and fries, Nan. And maybe some coffee."

"Coming right up," she smiled. While I waited for my food, I planned tomorrow's trip to Logansport. First, I needed to figure out how I was going to be free to roam around inside someone else's house hunting for a satchel hidden in a closet. If the satchel was there, it would be an easy case. I would get the money and another case would be closed.

I needed to call Nick. We've been friends since we were kids. His father was a real con man from the old days and taught his son the trade—how to keep secrets, how to tell the good guys from the bad guys, how to make false documents, who to sell them to, and who not to. I needed him to make me documents that would get me into the Erie Avenue house without raising any suspicions.

Nan brought over my food and I ate quickly, maybe too quickly. I finished my coffee, paid my bill, and left.

The following morning, I got up a little later than I

had planned and got ready to go to Logansport. I didn't even take time to eat; I would eat an early lunch with Nick. I grabbed my .38 Special with property of Spokane Police Dept. engraved on it and headed to Culver.

CHAPTER TWO

It was a nice quiet drive, and I got to Culver in good time. I was supposed to meet Nick at the A&W Root Beer Stand at the Culver beach. I arrived early, so I took a walk out on the pier. I was admiring Lake Maxinkuckee, the second largest lake in Indiana, when I saw him walk up. Nick was an easy-going guy, about six feet tall, and a bit scruffy looking. He had helped me on several cases and was easy to work with.

"Hi, Joe. Good to see you," he said, and handed me a cup of coffee.

"Thanks, Nick. It's good to see you, too. I was just admiring the lake. I never get tired of being out here." We walked along the beach for a bit, and caught up on each other's lives.

That brought us to the reason for today's meeting. We stepped across the highway and went inside the root beer stand. I ordered us a couple of root beer floats and burgers. We sat down with our food and ate while I told him more about the strange case I was working on.

When I got to the part about the house in Logansport, Nick took out a State Fire Marshall's badge and ID card and said that should get me access into the house to look around. We finished our food and exchanged goodbyes. He was an avid fisherman, so I promised to go out on the lake with him next time I was in town.

I took Hwy. 17, which was the back way to Logansport. Most people took Hwy. 31 because it was more of a direct route, bypassing small towns. But I needed time to think about my approach to the people that would open the door on Erie Avenue.

I was about three or four miles past the small town of Grass Creek when I got a flat on my brand new Camaro.

I pulled over in front of a two-story, white house on a small hill. There was an aged barn on the right side of the driveway. The paint was faded and some of the boards were missing. Chickens were pecking at the ground, and a teenage boy, about fifteen or sixteen, came out of the barn chasing a loose rabbit.

"Come on, Bugs," the teenage boy said. He looked up to see me. "Oh, wow! My favorite car," the boy exclaimed. "Can I help you with your flat?" he asked as he stared at the tire. "My name is Dennis." He was a friendly lad, about five foot ten, and had a good tan going. *It must have been from chasing that rabbit all day in the hot sun.*

"Sure, kid," I responded. I'll give you a dollar if you change my tire."

"Ok," Dennis said. "But it'll cost you another dollar to tighten the lug nuts."

"You run a hard bargain, Dennis, but it's a deal." After he changed my tire, tightened the lug nuts, and put the spare in the trunk, I handed him a five. His eyes lit up.

"Thanks, mister," Dennis said, and I was on my way.

I had driven about a mile when a young kid stuck out his thumb for a ride. I pulled over.

"Going to Logansport?" the kid asked.

"Yes," I said.

. "My name is Steve."

"I'm Joe."

"Glad to meet you, Joe. I have an appointment with my recruiter. I'm joining the Army."

"Good for you," I responded, thinking he looked pretty young. "Any good hotels in Logansport? I need to find a place to stay for a few days."

"Well, I work at the Captain Logan Hotel right downtown, just across the Eel River Bridge," Steve said.

"Sounds good. Is there a restaurant there?" "Yes, and a good coffee shop, a bar, and a theater a block down," Steve said. I dropped him off in front of the hotel. After parking my car on a side street, I registered and went upstairs to room 350. Good number.

After getting my belongings situated, I went down to eat and then had a drink in the bar before heading back to my room. I had barely walked into the room when I heard a knock at the door.

Two men in suits were standing there and introduced themselves as *interested parties*. One weighed about three hundred pounds and was six feet tall. The second guy was smaller—only two hundred pounds and barely five feet tall. The giant smelled of garlic, and said he knew I was after the treasure. They had been watching Mrs. Cryer and knew that I was working for her.

"Let me introduce myself. I'm George and this is my partner Rex. We've been hired to find and return the two million Bill Cryer stole. That's all we want."

"Who do you work for?" I asked.

"Henry Gueyser. Ever hear of him? It was his dough," said the big guy.

"*The* Henry Gueyser? The carmaker?" I managed to ask.

"Yes," said George.

"If I find you're telling the truth," I said, "and I do find the money, I will return it, minus fifteen percent. Ten for Mrs. Cryer and five for me"

"We can live with that. But don't think we're a couple of patsy's you can con. We have our eyes on you."

As the men started to leave, someone else knocked on the door. The two guys pushed their way past Steve who had come to check up on me. "Everything ok, Joe?" Steve asked.

"Yes. What brings you up here?"

"I wanted to make sure your room was okay."

"The room's great," I said. "By the way, Steve, is there a back way out of this hotel?"

"Sure is," Steve said. "Go to the coffee shop, through the swinging doors, take a left past the dishwasher, then down the hallway to the service door."

"Thanks," I said, clapping him on the shoulder.

"If there's anything you need, just ask for me. I'm easy to find," Steve offered as he turned to leave.

"I'll keep that in mind," I said.

Morning arrived after a good night's sleep. I decided I was going to have myself a good, strong cup of coffee and be on my way. I glanced at today's headlines. They were depressing—*George Romney Sends in National Guard to Stop Detroit Riots.*

I paid my bill and headed to the Erie Avenue house. It was a two-story, middle-class home that was freshly painted and in good repair. Time to use the phony name Nick gave me with the equally phony ID. I knocked on the door and a young couple answered.

"Hi, my name is Ralph Snyder. I'm with the State Fire Marshall's office doing a routine fire inspection. Is this a good time? It will only take a few minutes."

"Sure," the young man said, "as long as you can

prove who you are. Anticipating this exact question, I pulled out my ID and badge.

The young man looked at it carefully, smiled, and said, "Ok, come on in."

I took out my flashlight and looked in each room. First, I went into the living room, then the dining room, and finally the bedroom. The couple followed me around each room, not that I blamed them. I looked in the closet very carefully. No loose boards, no sign of a hidden panel. "Ok to look upstairs?" I asked.

"Sure thing," the young man said. I followed them up the stairs. The first bedroom on the right had a big closet.

"I'll have to crawl in there," I said, "and look for any potential fire hazards. I crawled into the closet and saw two rows of hanging clothes. On the other side of the second closet pole was another door. It opened into a second bedroom. *Very cool—a double closet.* There was nothing of interest there, so I stepped out into the hall.

"I'm in the other bedroom," I yelled to the young couple. *One more room to go.* I entered the last bedroom. It was smaller than the other bedrooms and had a small closet. On the right side was a narrow opening that ran along the length of the house. *Nothing but pipes down through these walls.* I shined my flashlight up, and I saw a long rope hanging from the pipes. I grabbed it carefully as it looked a little rotted. I pulled slowly. It felt heavy. I gave a tug and a small, brown leather satchel fell to the floor of the closet. My heart began to race. I quickly stuffed the satchel into my oversized jacket and quickly got out of the closet. I turned around to find the young couple staring at me. "Just checking the pipes," I said. "Everything looks good. You shouldn't need another inspection for at least five years."

I was anxious to see what sort of treasure was in this satchel, but I knew I couldn't look in it here. I got in my car and drove around town looking for a phone booth. I finally found one at the Post Office a few blocks away. I called the Captain Logan Hotel and asked for Steve.

"Hello?"

"Steve, this is Joe. Can you get me another room that I'm not registered under? I need it for about an hour."

"No. Mr. Mills, the owner, watches those house keys like a hawk. But I have a room here that you can use for as long as you need."

"I'm being watched, so I can't be seen with you," I said. "Can you hide the key somewhere in the bathroom by the lobby?"

"Sure thing," Steve said.

.A few minutes later, I walked into the hotel and headed straight to the bathroom. I looked around for the key. It took me a minute or two to find it. There was a good-sized lip under the sink big enough to hide a key—sure enough it was there. I headed up the back stairs to Steve's room. Surprisingly, it was clean and organized. He was off to a good start since the military was death on orderliness, I thought.

I sat down at the table, pulled the satchel out of my jacket, and dumped out its contents. The first thing I saw was a key. It was a heavy-duty key, not a safe deposit key, as I had seen plenty of those. It was a longer key—longer then any key I had ever seen. It was made of… no, not titanium. It couldn't be. I wasn't an expert in metals, but I could usually tell what kind of metal something was made of.

I then picked up an odd-shaped tool that looked like a socket of some sort. It was made of a type of crystal with about fifty grooves inside like it had been designed to fit tightly into some kind of lock. Now I was really puzzled.

The next item was a small bottle with a spray cap. It was full of liquid, but there was no label on the bottle saying what it was. It was just a white bottle full of something I didn't recognize.

I picked up a small notebook. On the first page was a riddle: "Between nine and ten, here I lie. All my friends surround me." *What was that supposed to mean?* On the next page there was a reference to the Blue Bar being the headquarters.

Headquarters for what? Maybe for the people who stole the two million from Henry Gueyser? The third and final written page was a note: "Jackie at the Blue Bar wants to see me."

Under the notebook was an old, silver Zippo lighter. There didn't appear to be anything special about it; it didn't even work when I tried to light it. I don't know why, but I removed the part that holds the lighter fluid. The cotton was gone and in its place was a piece of paper like you would find in a fortune cookie. Written on it was another riddle: "The three Indian trails will lead you to some of your answers." "The what?" I muttered to myself. "I can't catch a break. What Indian trails?"

There were also some fingernail clippers, a comb, and a wallet with two thousand dollars in it. I figured that was emergency get-out-of-town money.

There was also an ID card with Bill Cryer's picture on it. So, Mrs. Cryer was right. Something was fishy. Her husband must have been involved in the money heist. That was everything in the wallet and the satchel. I had just put it all back when there was a knock on the door. It was Steve.

"Hey, Joe. Those two men that were in your room last night are sitting in the lobby pretending to read the paper."

"Thanks, Steve. I'm done here. I appreciate the use of your room. Here's your key. Guess I'd better go talk to them."

As I put the satchel back in my suit jacket, I headed out the door, turned to him, and said, "I have a riddle for you, Steve. 'Between nine and ten, here I lie. All my friends surround me.' What do you think that means?"

After rubbing his chin for a second, Steve said, "Oh, that's easy. You'd have to be from here to know it, though. The old graveyard is between Ninth Street and Tenth Street. Erie Avenue and Spear Street are on the opposite sides, and in the middle of the cemetery is a small crypt that couldn't hold more then two coffins."

"That's it!" I pounded Steve on the back! *The money*

must be in the crypt! "Thanks Steve. I will make sure you are well-rewarded when I'm done with this case."

Now it was time to head downstairs to talk to the two guys in the lobby.

CHAPTER THREE

I headed downstairs and found George and Rex sitting in the lobby.

"Joe," Rex nodded a greeting. "Any new developments on our loot?"

I didn't want to spill all I knew, as I hadn't time to make sure these two clowns were legit. Besides, I was going to be the one who solved this case.

"I could use your help," I countered. "I think Bill and some guy named Jackie orchestrated this heist. Jackie either owns or works at the Blue Bar. I think we should go pay him a visit."

"You might be right," George said. "Let's go."

"Ok, meet you over there," Rex added.

"Let's all ride over in my Camaro," I suggested.

"No offense, Joe, but we're big guys and we need a lot of room. Let's go in my Cadillac," Rex insisted, pointing toward the alley. "Besides, it's parked right out back." So the three of us took off in the Cadillac with the beefy guys up front.

"The Blue Bar is supposed to be on 18th and Erie. Head a couple blocks south and then go east on Erie until we see it on the right," I directed.

About five minutes later, we arrived at the Blue Bar and went in. Two pool tables greeted us when we walked through the door. Just beyond them was a bar. There were tables to the right, and another room was to the left full of more tables, a dance floor, and a stage. We sat at the bar and ordered beers. After we finished drinking, we paid our tab and asked the bartender if Jackie was in.

"Are you salesmen?" the bartender asked.

"Sure," I said. "Salesmen. We have something for Jackie."

The bartender jerked his head to the right. "He's in his office on the other side of that jukebox." We headed to the office. The door was ajar, so George stepped in first.

"Can I help you?" Jackie said not so nicely.

"Yeah," Rex said. "I want to talk to you about Bill."

"Who's Bill?" Jackie asked.

I noticed that Jackie looked a lot like Rodney Dangerfield.

"Bill Cryer," I said.

"Never heard of him," Jackie sneered, eyeing the beef. "Why don't the three of you sit down and take a load off." We sat down at his desk that was cluttered with paper, wrappers, and a full ashtray.

"We know, and can prove it, that you and Bill heisted two million from Henry Gueyser's estate. All we want is the money back, or we call the police," I said.

Jackie didn't look the least bit ruffled. "What proof do you think you have that I had anything to do with some heist?"

"Bill left a note linking you to the job," I said.

Suddenly Jackie pulled out a German Luger. "Ok, guys. I guess I will have to add murder to my resume."

I quickly grabbed a handful of sand and butts from the ashtray and threw it in Jackie's face. His gun went off and nailed me in the side. I reached for my

.38 just as George grabbed him, so I hit him over the head with it. I really wanted to shoot him. He dropped to the floor and George put him in a headlock while Rex aimed his gun at him.

"Ok," Jackie said. "I'll tell you the truth. I stole the money. Bill and I know a girl named Nancy who works in the office at Gueyser's. She helped me in a couple of other heists. One evening, she was in one of the stalls in the restroom when two girls came in laughing about their dates. Well, one of the girls said, 'Remember, we have to be here at six a.m. when the contractor for the new plant picks up the two million. With all the tension in Detroit he doesn't want to deal with our banks. He will be here at six-thirty in a white truck with the number three written on the side. I don't know the driver, but he will say 'New plant.' When he does, I hand him the money.'"

Jackie winced as George squeezed tighter. "After the girls left, Nancy went back to her desk and called me. I knew I had to work fast. It was at least a four-hour drive to Michigan. Bill and I got there about eight at night. We drove around hunting for a used white truck. We finally found one in a car lot that was closed. Bill hot-wired it. We waited until morning, went to the Gueyser office, and then backtracked about half a mile. I blocked the road with my car and pretended to have car trouble. Bill had the truck hidden behind some blueberry bushes. We had walkie-talkies, so when the truck came into view I called Bill. He came up behind the truck after it stopped and rammed it until it went into the ditch, being careful not to do too much damage to the truck. I spray painted the number three on my truck and drove to the Detroit office. The two girls came out. I yelled, 'New plant,' they handed me the money, and we were gone. We dumped the truck on our way home. We couldn't believe it was that easy.

"We nearly made it home, but I had a diabetic attack and Bill rushed me to the hospital. I told him to hide the money where we usually do in the closet at the Erie Avenue house. My younger sister lives there with her new husband. They have no clue what we do. I stay in that room sometimes when I work late. Anyway, the money wasn't there the next day and Bill was in jail in Plymouth. I watched his house but didn't dare go to the jail. When he got out, I went over to his house, but he had a heart attack before I could talk to him."

By this time, I was about to faint from the gunshot wound. Someone must have called the police because they showed up, and Rex explained to them what had happened. They took Jackie away, and an ambulance came for me. The paramedic said I only had a surface wound, so he cleaned it up, put on some sort of salve, and wrapped it up good. He talked to the doctor on his radio and told me there was a prescription waiting for me at the RX. He gave me some antibiotics and made me drink some nasty orange juice and said if I feel an infection coming on to call a doctor. I said I would, thanked him, and went back to where George and Rex were waiting.

"Well, looks like we're back to square one," Rex said.

They gave me a ride back to the hotel. "We'll check on you in a couple of days," George said.

I got out of the car and said, "Sorry it didn't work out," and headed to my room.

I wrote down the license plate number of George's car to give to Nick. I was sure he could find something on these guys. I called Nick and gave him the information. I then called the front desk and asked if they could send Steve up. Fifteen minutes later, he knocked on the door.

"Hi, Joe. You don't look so good. What do you need?"

"Hi, Steve. Could you go to the RX and pick up a prescription for me?"

"Sure," Steve said. I handed him a fifty and told him to keep the change.

"Thanks, Joe!" Steve pocketed the money and was off.

I decided to go to the coffee shop and have a bite to eat. I ordered the hot turkey sandwich with mashed potatoes. It was as good as Steve said it was. I paid my bill and started to get up, but the pain in my side was more then I could bear. I hurt too much to drive so I took a cab to the local hospital. The cabby pulled up close to the Emergency Room door and walked me in.

After the paperwork was done, there was nothing to do but wait on a very uncomfortable chair. It seemed like forever, but finally a candy striper called my name. She was very friendly— couldn't have been more then 15.

"Joe? I'm Sherry. Come with me." She took me to a private room and said the nurse would be right with me. True to her words, the young girl returned shortly with the nurse.

"Hi, Joe, I'm Beth. I'll be taking care of you. Let's get those bandages off and see what's going on. Just what I expected—a little infection starting. It's not too bad, though. Did you get that prescription filled?" she asked looking at my chart.

"It's being filled now," I said, barely able to keep my

head up.

"Sherry will stay with you while I go get you a booster shot. Then I'll put a new dressing on that wound."

While I was waiting for her to return, I noticed a picture on the wall. It was of a graduating class at Baker Street Academy. One of the names was Jimi Cryer. The year was 1950.

By this time, Nurse Beth was back with a needle. Luckily, she gave me the booster shot in the arm. I thanked them both and called a cab to take me back to the hotel. I went straight to my room where I found a prescription bottle on the nightstand and some money. There was a note from Steve that said the medicine only cost fifty cents, so he only took the change to take his girlfriend to the movies. Jules Vern's new movie, *Rocket to the Moon,* was playing. I got a glass of water, took two of my pills and crashed.

CHAPTER FOUR

I woke the following morning to the phone ringing.

"Yeah?" I said in my finest morning voice.

"Joe, this is Nick. I have some news for you on that license plate number I had my police buddy run. The car is registered to a George Brill at 820 Wallace Road, Detroit, Michigan. He's also a private detective. But that's not all. I just made an inquiry at the Logansport police station. You won't believe this, but two guys in Payroll at Gueyser Headquarters had fictitious employees on the payroll. Gueyser had been paying them for two years. The employees got paid in cash, so there were no bank records to deal with. They gave these bogus employees fairly large salaries, but not so large that it would cause questions. They managed to collect that two million in less then two years."

"Wow! So there never was a new plant?" I asked.

"Oh, there was a new plant being built, but not by those fake employees! Anyway, the IRS was getting suspicious because these nonexistent employees were not filing any tax returns. The two guys in Payroll knew this and had those two girls be their mule. They planned to skip town with the money and live in Canada. But now they are in police custody."

"Nick," I said looking at the photo on the wall, "how would you like to give me a tour of the Baker Street Academy today?"

"Sure thing, Joe. I'm not doing anything," Nick replied.

"Great. See you in about an hour." I got dressed, made a trip to the coffee shop, and downed several cups of coffee in about fifteen minutes. I needed some good strong coffee to keep me going. I headed out to the parking lot across the street from the hotel. A nice, older man in a booth greeted me. I told the man I was a guest at the hotel and would pay my parking bill when I checked out.

"No need," the gentleman said. "The hotel pays your parking."

I got in my Camaro and headed for Culver. It only took about half an hour to get to Nick's. He had a nice home on Baker Street. He met me at the door and asked if I would like a beer.

"Sounds great, thanks." We sat on the covered porch and talked about Culver. As Nick was sharing the history of Baker Street Academy, I took out the satchel and dumped its contents on the table.

"What's all this?" Nick asked. I explained how I found the satchel using the fake ID he had given me. Nick picked up the bottle and sprayed some on his hands. "This is luminal. It picks up protein and blood stains that you can't see. You spray it on an area and then you can see the stains you couldn't see before. He then picked up a piece of paper and read, "The three Indian trails will lead you to some of your answers."

"I know where those trails are, Joe. We used to play there when we were kids. They're on the way to the Academy. Why don't we walk the trails instead of driving there?" Nick suggested. We headed down toward the beach, but veered to the left where there was a stand of trees.

"The trails go through the trees, Joe. And here they are." Nick had a smile on his face. "The cadets would use the lower trail when they were going to swim at the public beach. They used the middle one if they were going to the park. And when they wanted to go to town, they walked along the top one."

We started on the top trail and had walked for a few minutes when I saw a girl about seventeen sitting under a tree reading a book. She looked up and smiled. I smiled back.

"Odd place to read a book," Nick commented curiously.

"I know," she said, "but it's so quiet here. Hardly anyone ever uses this trail. By the way, my name is Pam."

Nick introduced the two of us then said, "Well, we'll let you get back to your reading," I said. "It was nice meeting you, Pam."

She nodded to us and returned to her book.

We turned back to the trail when we heard her say softly, "And Joe, your answers lie ahead." When I turned around to ask her what she meant, she was gone.

The answers lie ahead. Wow, this case just got stranger. How would she know about that? As we walked along the trail, Nick continued with the history of the Academy. We stopped at one of the main halls and decided to check it out. There were lots of pictures on the walls, some dating back to the

1920s. There were photo albums on the tables, so I decided to sit down and look at some of them. Even though it was a fairly short walk, I was still feeling pretty weak from my wound. Halfway through the album, I got a chill clear up my spine, and it wasn't from the gash in my side. "Nick, look at this picture."

Nick, who was looking at the photos on the wall, came over to take a look. "Incredible!" he said. "That's the girl who was reading on the trail. Pam. But it couldn't be; this picture is from 1939."

The photo was of a teen-aged blonde girl standing next to a cadet. The caption under it identified the two as Jimi Cryer and Pam Cryer. A staff member came in and introduced herself as Jill. She asked if she could be of any help, so I asked her if she knew anything about the people in the picture.

"That's funny," Jill said not smiling. "I had only been working here for about six weeks when these two kids just disappeared. They were such good kids—always laughing and having a good time. "Anyway, there was a big search for them. The entire town came out to join in, but no luck. There weren't even any clues to go on. Then about a week later, their dad called off the search saying they had come home. He said they had run away because they were mad at him. Their parents removed them from the Academy and we never saw them again. Case closed, but a lot of us were left wondering what really happened."

I decided to borrow the picture from the album. I slipped it into my suit jacket and then went through a few more of the albums. There was another picture of Jimi Cryer. This time he was alone, standing in his Academy uniform in front of a house. "Jimi at Spear Street, Logansport, 1939" was the caption beneath the photo. I decided to borrow that picture too.

After looking around for a bit, we decided to leave and walked back to Nick's place. We talked about the strange events of the day and wondered if or what the Cryer kids had to do with our case.

Back at Nick's, we watched a baseball game—Yankees vs. Red Sox. Of course, the Yankees won 9 to 7. Nick was going to cook up some steaks, but I offered to take him to a steakhouse instead.

"My treat," I offered.

"If you're buying, I'm going!"

CHAPTER FIVE

We arrived at the steak house and were seated almost immediately. I noticed Pam, the girl we had seen earlier. She was with another girl—Sherry from the hospital. I watched in disbelief. They headed out the door before I could comprehend it all. They got into a white sedan and quickly sped away. The driver looked like Jimi from the picture. My mind was whirling. *What is going on? Maybe that medicine is really getting to me.* I wasn't sure how all of this was connected, but I knew it was. I would have to watch and see how it all played out.

We enjoyed our steaks while Nick talked about fishing. He invited me to go with him tomorrow to Bass Lake. He already had a cabin rented and had plenty of fishing poles and bait, so I wouldn't need to bring a thing. I accepted his offer, hoping the break would clear my head; I just hoped it wouldn't be too hard on my wounded side.

Two hours later, we were back at Nick's place, and since we needed to get an early start, he decided to hit the sack right away. Nick pointed out the guest room and said goodnight. I decided to watch TV for a while. I was watching a show on global events that I liked to watch whenever I could catch it. Tonight's episode was a speech by Hitler in the1930s. The crowd was cheering, and there was a close-up of two girls. I couldn't believe my eyes. Those two girls looked just like Pam and Sherry. I'm good at figuring out things, good at putting random details together and making sense out of them. But this case was way beyond anything I had ever been involved in.

The next thing I knew, Nick was waking me up. "You sleep out here all night, Joe? It's 5 a m." When I opened my eyes I saw that the TV was still on, but only noisy snow showed on the screen. "We need to leave in half an hour," he said.

I always carried a small suitcase in my car for emergencies like this. Half an hour later, after a quick shower and a bad cup of coffee, we were on the road to Bass Lake. We arrived by six and went into the general store to pick up our cabin keys. The man working the counter was Fredrick. "How can I help you?" he asked, glancing up from the case he was filling with lures.

"My name is Nick and I have a cabin reserved."

"Oh, yeah," Fredrick said, rubbing his chin. He reached up on the wall behind the counter and grabbed some keys hanging from a nail. "Cabin six is out the door on your right just past the dock."

After the paperwork was completed, we headed to the cabin. It had two bedrooms, a kitchen, and a room that doubled as a living room and dining room. We finished up quickly and were soon out on the lake with fishing poles in the water. Bass Lake is a very small Northern Indiana community. Only a couple thousand folks live here, Nick had said. Beautiful country.

Nick's bobber started to move slowly at first and then picked up speed. Bam! There it went. Nick pulled in a nice-sized bass. Soon Nick's pole was in the water again. Bam! Another nice Bass. I looked at him dumbfounded.

"Well," I said, "Two is all we need. No sense being greedy. I guess you get bragging rights."

"You bet I do," Nick said.

"That means you get to clean them, young man." I said. "I want to see if you can pull in some baked potatoes and sour cream to go along with the fish." At this point, nothing would surprise me.

"Did that already. The sour cream's in the fridge and

the bakers are wrapped and ready to go."

"Well, aren't you the organized one," I remarked. We both laughed and went on to shore. I turned on the oven to get the bakers started and made the garlic butter to drizzle over the fish while Nick cleaned them. Nick saw some fresh tomatoes in a basket on the porch next door and offered to buy two of them. The lady just handed them to him and told him to enjoy them. I sliced the tomatoes and set them on the table with salt and pepper. Half an hour later we were both eating.

"Boy, that was good," we said simultaneously,

"Jinx! You owe me a coke," I said.

"How about a beer instead?" Nick laughed. "Sounds good," I said. We were both too full to move so we chatted about the hardware store he owned in South Bend. Nick had inherited the store but didn't want to move there. He didn't need the money so he leased the store to a manager that had been there for twenty years. He got thirty percent of the profit. Nick admitted he could make more if he worked it, but it wasn't his thing. He didn't want to sell it because if something happened he always had that to fall back on.

There was no TV in the cabin and it was still early,

so we walked down to the general store and played a little pinball; the store had the new Diamond Jack machine. We played three games. I won two, Nick one. "Guess I have bragging rights now," I smiled.

"That you do," Nick agreed.

"Nick, I need to go back to Plymouth tomorrow to talk to Mrs. Cryer. It would be faster for me if you could go with me. Then I wouldn't have to back track."

"Sure," Nick said. "I'll go, but I'll drop you off. I need to do some errands in Plymouth that will take about an hour. When I finish, I'll pick you up."

"Perfect." I replied.

Next morning we were off to Plymouth. Nick turned on the radio and Neil Diamond's song *Solitary Man* was playing. When the song finished, the Alka Seltzer commercial came on, Plop, plop, fizz, fizz..."

"Now for the news," the announcer said. "A rare blue diamond was found today by a homeless man in the Bronx. Authorities were notified when the man tried to sell it at Tiffany's. No word yet as to who will get possession of the diamond. We'll keep you notified. I'll be rooting for the homeless man. Now Roy Orbison's *Pretty Woman*."

Tuning out the music, Nick commented, "Wow, why can't we get that lucky, Joe?"

"I know," I said.

As we came to a four-way stop, I noticed a convertible speed by. It looked like Pam and Sherry with Jimi driving. *This is starting to be more then a coincidence.* Nick dropped me off at Mrs. Cryer's and then sped off. She answered the door on my first knock.

"Well, hello, Joe. It's been a few days. How are you doing on the case?"

"Well, Mrs. Cryer, that's what I came here to talk to you about. We found out that your husband was involved in a robbery. Two million dollars to be exact."

"I know, Joe. The police were here and they questioned me for hours. They had a search warrant. So many cops, Joe. I'm still trying to clean up after them," Mrs. Cryer cried softly. "They searched and searched but couldn't find anything. I tried to get hold of you but you didn't leave a number.

"Sorry, Mrs. Cryer. I'll leave a phone number where you can reach me. I have another question for you. Did you have any children?"

"Oh, heavens no, Joe. We never did."

"Do you have a place where you could hide things that even the police would miss?"

"Yes, my husband took out the old wall heaters and made a safe box out of them. You have to pull off the paneling to get to it."

"May I take a look?" I asked.

"Certainly," she agreed. She took me to the guest bedroom where, after a little work, I was finally able to pop open the paneling. There was a hole one foot by one foot. In it was a small box. There was no money, only some papers that were of no value to me. I shoved the box back in and heard a snap. I pulled the box back out and another door appeared. I reached in to find another box the same size. I opened it to find a picture of a huge machine. The machine had twelve seats like a roller coaster and dials with dates on them. There were no pedals but it had a lever where the steering wheel should be. The picture looked like it was taken in a dungeon. There appeared to be a lot of items around it, but I couldn't tell what they were.

There was also a picture of two men in a laboratory with weird shaped objects made of materials I had never seen before. Some guy was in the corner holding an object to his ear and talking to himself.

There was another picture with a group of twelve people smiling for the camera, and there amongst them was Pam, Sherry, Jimi, and Bill. I didn't recognize the other eight. I found an envelope with a small crystal in it and a note that said, "If you lose your way, place this crystal on the hand of the crypt." I didn't know what that meant but decided to pocket the envelope and pictures. Nothing else seemed of any value—just some stamps, loose staples, and old cobwebs. I put the box back in the safe, just a bit disappointed and a lot curious. I couldn't believe there was another riddle to solve.

"Was it of any help, Joe?"

"Maybe, Mrs. Cryer. I'm not sure yet." I pulled out the picture that I borrowed from the Culver Military Academy. "Do any of these people look familiar to you?"

"Oh, yes! All three. They were my husband's friends. They would sit in the drawing room and talk for hours."

"What did they talk about, Mrs. Cryer?"

"Well, I don't really know. I would bring them tea and leave them alone. Whenever I came back into the room, they would either stop talking or change the subject."

"Surely, Mrs. Cryer, you must have heard something."

"Well, I did hear them say once that some commander had said, 'It is time for you to return. You are twenty-five years late and your replacement is ready.' I asked my husband about it, and he said it was just a play Jimi had seen and that he was reenacting some of it. Funny, but that was the last time I saw any of them, and that was a year ago."

There was a knock on the door and it was Nick. "Ready to go, Joe?" he asked.

"Sure thing." I said. "Well, Mrs. Cryer, I'll be in touch."

"OK, Joe. Thank you so much for stopping."

"Oh, before I forget, here's my hotel phone number. If you call, the hotel will let me know." Mrs. Cryer took the paper and we left.

CHAPTER SIX

Nick still had the radio on as we drove back to Culver. I caught myself humming to the music while Nick was tapping his fingers on the steering wheel. Then the local news came on.

"The police are still puzzled over the whereabouts of the stolen two million from the Gueyser payroll office in Detroit. For national news, President Johnson visits the graveside of President Kennedy. A rare 1921 Bentley was discovered in a grocery store parking lot in the Bronx. As of this moment, no one seems to know who the owner is, but the police have it in special storage. The owner has ninety days to claim it before it goes to auction. What's up in the Bronx lately? That's it for me. Stay tuned for the *Rockin' Rick Show*."

"Wow, we really need to move to the Bronx," I said.

"No kidding," muttered Nick.

We pulled up to Nick's house. Both of us were very tired. "I need to get back to Logansport, Nick. You don't mind if I take off do you?"

"As much as I enjoy your company, Joe, I need a nap."

"Ok," I said. "I'll keep in touch."

The trip back to Logansport was quick in my new Camaro. I parked my car, and Douglas, the elderly parking lot attendant, waved me over.

"Lots of strange things going on," Douglas said.

"What do you mean?" I asked.

"I spend a few minutes talking to the regulars who come in here. Almost all of them tell me items that were lost for years have just reappeared. One man told me he was getting a box off the shelf in his closet when he saw his grandfather's wallet just lying there. It still had money in it—a twenty, two fives and a bunch of ones. All the bills were from the 1920s. Another man's new bicycle that disappeared forty years ago was on his front porch. It looked just like it did when it disappeared! The news is saying that people all over the country are finding things that, years ago, had been either lost or stolen. Is that strange or what?" the old man said. "All in one night. I think the end is near."

I was just as puzzled thinking about the items found in the Bronx. I walked over to the hotel where I saw Steve putting letters onto an events board.

He looked over and said, "Hi, Joe. You have some messages. George and Rex want you to call them. Here's the number they gave me."

As Steve paused, I said, "You said messages?" "Oh, right." A Mrs. Cryer called and said her dead husband was missing and for you to call her right away. That's it." Steve said.

"He might be right," I muttered to myself.

"Who might be right?" questioned Steve.

"Old man Douglas. He said the end was near."

I gave Steve a five, thanked him, and headed up to my room. I began thinking that I needed to get to the graveyard soon and have a look at that crypt, but I'd better not do it alone. If I have any trouble it would be nice to have backup. Nick would be in South Bend for a few days, so that left him out. I'll worry about that later. Right now I needed to make some phone calls. First I called Mrs. Cryer, who was frantic.

"Joe," Mrs. Cryer cried, "I have been making

arrangements for my husband's funeral for the last four days. All the time they kept trying to get me to have his body cremated. I kept refusing, and today they admitted they had lost my husband."

"I'm so sorry," I said, "but how does a funeral home go about losing a body?"

"I don't know, Joe," Mrs. Cryer replied. "The police are investigating it. There isn't much I can do."

"Well, let me know what you hear. I'll keep checking things on my end," I said. I hung up and dialed the number Steve had given me. Rex answered the phone

"Rex here. How can I help you?"

"It's Joe. I got your message."

"I have a tip on the case. It seems Bill frequented a local lake in Logansport known by the locals as Kenneth Lake. He always had a certain spot where he would go swimming. People would be worried because he would go down under the water but they would never see him come back up. The only information I could get was that it was somewhere in the northwest corner of the lake."

"Thanks, Rex. I'll check that out," I said.

"Oh, and Joe, remember that if you find the money

the reward is fifteen percent," Rex said.

"And if you find it first its the same," I reminded him.

"Of course, of course," Rex assured me, and we both hung up.

I called up front. "Front desk," an older woman answered. "This is Jan. How can I assist you?"

"Hi," I said. May I speak to Steve?"

"One moment, please. He's busy hanging up an activity board," Jan replied. After what seemed like hours but was really only minutes, Steve answered the phone.

"This is Steve. How may I help you?"

"This is Joe. Are you busy this afternoon?"

"I'm afraid I am, Joe. I'm working a double and won't be off until midnight. I won't get off until the graveyard shift arrives. But I'm off tomorrow. What is it you need?"

"Are you familiar with Kenneth Lake?"

"I sure am. I go there all the time with my girlfriend."

"Could you give me a tour of the lake tomorrow? I'll pay you for your time."

"Sure thing. What time?"

"How about eleven? That will give you time to sleep in. Just call my room when you're ready."

"Ok. See you tomorrow."

I decided to go see a movie since I couldn't do much until tomorrow. I walked down to the local theatre where a new movie, *Cool Hand Luke* starring Paul Newman and George Kennedy, was playing. It was a great movie. *I don't ever recall seeing a bad movie with either Paul Newman or George Kennedy.*

I went back to the hotel and stopped at the bar and chatted with the bartender while I had a drink. Most of the patrons had their eyes on the baseball game that was playing. Every once-in-a-while, I would hear someone say that the umpire needed glasses, that Mickey was out at first base, or that guy couldn't hit a baseball if it were a basketball. Then Horace hit a home run and everyone started laughing and the loud guy shut up.

I had one more drink then headed back to my room. I turned on the ten o'clock news. They were talking about how people as far away as Alaska suddenly found lost items of value. Then they went on to say that a funeral home was under investigation for losing a body. The theory was that the body had accidentally been cremated. The weather report said that tomorrow was supposed to be in the eighties. That was good.

CHAPTER SEVEN

The next morning I put on my swimming trunks, dressed over them, and met Steve in the lobby. "Got your trunks on, Steve?" I asked.

"Sure do," he said, adjusting his jeans.

"We need to stop at a hardware store first. Steer me in the right direction. Tell you what, Steve, you just drive. We'll save a lot of time since you know the way and I don't."

"For real?"

"Why not?" I smiled.

Steve got behind the steering wheel of my new car and said "Wow" over and over. He was being a bit too cautious for my taste and I assured him that the car could go faster and that it was fully insured.

"You don't have to tell me twice," Steve grinned. He looked in both mirrors and floored it.

"Now that's what I'm talking about." I chuckled. We were soon at the hardware store. I bought a hundred-foot rope, a pocketknife for each of us, and a very large first-aid kit. Then we were off to Kenneth Lake. Once there, I noticed that it was almost all covered by cliffs except for a small beach area where families were gathered enjoying the sun and water.

"Steve," I said. "I want to go to the northwest corner. What's the easiest way to get there?"

"Well," Steve said looking out at the water. "We need to go around the lake from up here. There's a path that goes all the way around.

Fifteen minutes later we were at a spot I thought was perfectly northwest or close to it. We must have been right because Steve found a trail going down to the water. The problem was that you needed one hand to hold onto the rocks while going down so you wouldn't slip. I carried the rope and flashlight, Steve grabbed the first-aid kit, and we slowly made our descent.

Once we were at the bottom, I explained to Steve that I was going to tie the rope around myself. We needed to find a rock big enough to wrap the other end of the rope around. I told him he would need to give me about thirty feet of loose rope. If I tugged on it, he would need to pull me in. Steve said he understood, so I took a deep breath and went under. The water was pretty clear and I had no trouble seeing. I was down only about six feet, so I went a little deeper. I still did not find anything. I wasn't sure how deep the lake was; I thought maybe Bill had put the money in something waterproof and tied it to a rock, but surely any current would have moved it, so I knew I needed to look for something tied to the side of the cliff. I was running out of breath so I pulled on the rope and Steve quickly pulled me up much faster then I could have done on my own.

"I think I need to go deeper," I said. "Give me ten more feet on the rope, Steve."

He estimated ten more feet by using his own height. By then, I was breathing well again. The second time I went a little deeper. I was about 12 feet under. I shined my flashlight at the cavern walls. They glistened in the light, and I saw a few small paddlefish swimming my way. *But they seemed to be coming from inside the wall*. As I shined the light directly at the fish, I saw an opening. It looked like an underground cave. Nearly out of breath, I pulled on the rope once again. Up to the task, Steve pulled me in. After getting my breath, I explained to Steve that there was an underground cave about twelve feet down. I asked him if he would like to explore it with me.

"I sure would," Steve said. I'm a really good swimmer and can stay underwater for a long time."

"Good," I said. "We won't be using a rope and we only have one flashlight."

"What if we cut the rope in half so both of us can tie off?" Steve suggested. "It will be a little slower but safer. Plus twelve feet is a cinch. So if we can breathe in the cave we should be fine. A little leery, I agreed. Steve cut the rope with the new pocketknife, and boy was it sharp.

"Thanks for the knife, Joe," Steve said.

"You're welcome," I said while tying the rope around my waist. "You can still back out, Steve. I won't think any less of you."

"Oh, no. I'm going." Steve said eagerly. We both took deep breaths and went in. Swimming to the cave was easy. We were there in less then a minute. Once inside, Steve and I went to the surface and took a good deep breath. There was a ceiling about eight feet above our heads. We swam about twenty more feet until we came to an area not covered in water. It was about fifty feet high and one hundred feet wide. My flashlight struggled to illuminate enough of the cave to see what all was there.

We both got to dry ground where I noticed a sleeping bag and some cooking utensils. There were pockets in the walls of the cave where Bill had been storing things. Steve found a large wooden crate filled with candles of all sizes. He took out several, lit them, and placed them around the cave. He noticed the flame flickering toward the south, so he knew there was plenty of oxygen coming into the cave. Another box had rations that you would find in an emergency shelter: a two pound metal can of dried eggs, powdered mashed potatoes, crackers, and even a cake. There seemed to be enough food to last one person for at least three months.

Steve took a lit candle and wandered around the cave. "Joe, over here," Steve called.

I followed the sound of Steve's voice and was amazed at what he had found. It was a generator—not a small one but a big one half the size of my car.

"I think it works," he said pointing to the on/off button. I pushed it, but it just sputtered. I checked for gas and it was full, so I tried again. This time it sputtered a second and then fired. Lights began to flicker and soon the whole cave lit up.

"Unbelievable!" I said, turning off the now unnecessary flashlight. As I looked around, I saw that the cave resembled a deserted village. There had to be fifty gallons of gas, and there was a box filled with underwater flashlights. I grabbed two flashlights and tossed one to Steve. There were cases and cases of food. Bill had his own survival store here. In two of the wall pockets, I found beds. *Was Bill expecting company?* Steve found a world radio with reception. *How was that even possible down here?* Looking in another of the pockets, Steve found a cash box with about two thousand dollars in new one hundred dollar bills. He showed me the money, and I said, "Well, if no one claims the money, Steve, it's yours."

"Cool." answered Steve with a look of hope on his face.

That was all the money we found—but not the two million we were hoping was here.

"Steve, I said, "There must be another way out. Bill couldn't have brought all this stuff down here by diving in the water." He agreed. So we searched the walls for an opening. I noticed one of the pockets had another pocket above it. As I looked up at the pocket ceiling, which was about six feet above our heads, I noticed an elevator lift. *But how do you get it down?*

Steve must have noticed my puzzled look because he said, "Its simple, Joe. There are ropes and pulleys on the lift and a lever slowly lowers you down."

"But we're down here and the lift is up there, I commented. "And the walls are too slippery to climb."

"I know. That's why we have this," Steve said, showing me a fifteen-foot pole with a round hook on the end. "I grew up on a farm where we used to put hay in the loft. This was how it was done." He put the hook onto the lever of the lift and it slowly came down. Steve stopped it about two feet from the ground.

"Well, I'll be." I said.

"After you, Joe", Steve said. I got on to the lift with Steve following close behind. He tugged on the pulley. Hearing the moaning sounds of the ropes and the jingling of the pulleys, I thought it sounded like a bad rock band. Soon we were in the top pocket looking down at the water and surrounding island.

"Joe," Steve said, "we didn't shut off the generator and our ropes are down there."

"That's ok," I said turning around to see we were in another room. "We could use the light. This room is lit up and I'm sure it's the generator that's providing it. Besides, it will shut off when it runs out of gas."

"How much longer do you think we have before it shuts off?" Steve asked.

"Well, if it was full, about another hour." I replied.

I went first. These cavern walls were much dryer. The cavern made so many twists and turns, and ups and downs that I was getting dizzy. Steve, however, was smiling from ear to ear.

"Best adventure I have ever been on," Steve said gleaming.

"Glad you're enjoying yourself," I said. The walls were getting wider and up ahead was a good-sized boulder leaning against the wall floor. "Let's rest a while. I'm getting tired and hungry. We sat on the boulder and Steve reached into a bag he had found in the lower cave and handed me a few crackers and cheese in a small metal container.

"What's this?" I asked.

"I was a Boy Scout," Steve remarked.

"Remind me to thank you later," I said, grabbing the crackers and cheese. "Not bad." Ten minutes later we were off again.

"I think we're going uphill now, Steve. It's getting steeper." The cave soon began to level out and the walls got narrower—only about four feet on each side. I could smell the damp, musty cave walls. "How far do you think we've gone?"

"Well," Steve said, stopping a moment to think, "There's 5,280 feet in a mile and I counted almost 5,000 feet with a length of about two feet per stride. I guess we've walked about two miles."

I spun around. "You've been counting every step since we started?" I asked dumbfounded. "That's incredible. You *are* a Boy Scout! I think you deserve a promotion." I continued taking the lead and, according to Steve, we walked about half a mile further. The cave ended and a wooden door met me in the face. I wasn't expecting a door in the cave, and I wondered if I should open the door or knock on it. Just then the lights went out.

"I guess the generator is out of gas," Steve said, He quickly turned on his flashlight so I could see the door. I don't think I've ever been in such a dark space, and I was surprised at how much light just one small flashlight could produce. I tried the door and it was unlocked. I opened it slowly and turned on my flashlight as well. It appeared that we were in a basement.

We looked around. There was a coal furnace, shelves along the wall, an old sink, and a pile of coal that was so old I thought they would soon become diamonds. We found a staircase at the end of the basement, so we decided to continue on up to see where they went. They lead us to another unlocked door that opened into a kitchen. As we entered, I could see it was in terrible disrepair. The cupboard doors were hanging loose and the red and green wallpaper was faded and torn. There wasn't much in the way of furnishings anywhere in the house that would tell us anything about who had lived there. We were ground level, and when I looked out the window I could see the countryside was mostly farmland. There was a road about 250 feet from the house. We had forgotten we were still in our wet swimming trunks and were feeling the chill of the damp old house. We stepped out onto the rickety porch and the sun felt good on our wet bodies. I glanced down and was surprised at how dirty we were. We looked as though we were on the losing end of a mud-wrestling contest.

"Do you know where are, Steve?" I asked.

"Yes, we're not too far from where we started. We're out on the back road to the lake. No one uses it much any more. This is how the locals used to get in to swim. Years ago there wasn't a front way in. It was all private land. Follow me," he said. We walked along the old highway and only a few cars drove by. My guess was that mostly the locals used it, and what a sight they were getting today. A car full of girls drove by laughing "Woohoo!" at us. Steve seemed to be enjoying my embarrassment when I asked him how much longer we were going to be walking in public like this.

Laughing, he said that we would be leaving the road in just a moment.

"It will be rough going for a bit," he said. We need to make our way through a lot of overgrown bushes and thistles."

The only reply from me was one "ouch" after the other.

"You need to go barefoot more often," Steve said with a laugh.

"Very funny," I said, picking my way carefully. Once again we were at the top of the cliffs. It didn't take us long to get down to where we had left our clothes. We both took about a ten-minute swim to wash off the mud and then let the warm sun dry us off before we dressed and headed back to the hotel.

"Hey, Steve," I said, "is it ok with you if we keep that

cave a secret for now?"

"That's fine with me. I always wanted my own secret cave." We had a good laugh and decided we were hungry. Back at the hotel, I offered to buy Steve dinner.

"One of the perks of working here is that I get money for my meals," Steve laughed. "So dinner is on me."

After we finished eating, Steve went back to his room, but I needed a drink so I headed to the bar. I was tired. Really tired. I couldn't remember the last time I had walked so much. I was beginning to nod off when the news caught my attention.

"People are still finding items that were lost years ago. One car salesman told me that ten Model T's came in just today. The cars just appeared in front of the owners' homes. They said these old cars had belonged to their grandparents years ago and had been stolen. They were never found until now. I'm standing live in front of an antique store where people are lined up around the block trying to sell old items that were just discovered in their houses, garages, and basements. One man told me he found an early 1800s book collection in his son's tree house. The collection was his great-grandfather's. I talked to the owner of the antique shop and was told they could be put out of business if it keeps up. Too many of the same antiques could make values plummet. This is Peggy Larson reporting for KOTT."

Dumbfounded, I finished my drink and went to my room. Before hitting the sack, I decided to make a few phone calls. One was to George and Rex explaining the lake was a bust, which was partially true, as we hadn't found the money. I was thinking that there were two stashes. Bill had one at Erie Avenue and one at the lake. And were there more? And why hide the money? Was something going to happen where he needed to get away quickly?

I was still puzzled about the conversation that Mrs. Cryer had overheard about replacements being ready. *What did that mean?* It was too much for me to think about right now. I would do a quick walk through the old graveyard tomorrow. And my other phone calls could wait. Now for some sleep.

CHAPTER EIGHT

I woke up late, which was ok because I didn't have much planned for today. I went down to the lobby and paid my bill. I told the clerk at the counter that I would be staying on for a while, and then I went to the coffee shop and had some pancakes and coffee.

Steve dropped by, "Hi, Joe, what a day yesterday was. "Yeah," I replied. "Thanks again for the supper last night."

"No problem," he nodded. "I need to get back to work, but I just wanted to stop by and say hi."

I overheard two men in a suit talking about the old graveyard and their plans to expand it. "We can go two hundred yards on two sides," one man said, "which would bring in a lot of money. First, we would have to buy the houses, though, and demolish them. That could be expensive."

The other man remarked that all of the houses were owned by one man. "We have a meeting next week with the owner. He doesn't seem very eager to sell, so it might cost us too much unless we can get the city council to help us." My attention was interrupted by the waitress offering me more coffee.

"No thanks," I said. I turned around and the two men were gone. That's a lot of houses for one person to own, I thought. I left the diner and drove to the old cemetery. I looked at all the worn gravestones, many of which were from the 1800s.

I moved swiftly through the graveyard when I noticed Pam and Sherry up ahead.

"Hi girls."

Both girls turned around startled, "Oh, hi." said Sherry. "How is your wound?"

"Pretty much healed," I said. "Thanks for asking."

"You look familiar," Pam said.

"I met you in Culver on the Indian trails," I said.

"That's' right," Pam said nodding. "We were just visiting our grandparents. We're sisters. We live in different towns so it's nice when we can get together."

"You bet," I said.

"Are you visiting relatives?" Sherry asked.

"No, just taking a shortcut."

"Well, we should go. Bye, Joe."

I nodded my head and watched the girls as they left. They went inside a house near the cemetery. It was odd that they lived so close. I continued looking around, and I finally found the crypt. It was a tall marble crypt, not too big. Maybe four people could fit inside. Attached to the outside of it was a stone cherub with both hands cupped; her hands were full of fresh bird food. When I moved away, a robin landed on her fingers and began eating.

The crypt had no information as to who was interred. It wasn't locked, but I didn't want to go in alone; I wanted to wait for Nick. I decided to stake out the cemetery and the house where the girls had gone. I went to the store and bought a soda and then drove back to Tenth Street and parked.

I was listening to the radio when the announcer came on. "No one seems to be finding lost items today. I guess it's a slow day in the lost and found department. This is Charlie with the latest news." I shut off the radio; I just needed some quiet time.

About an hour later, the two girls came out. They got into a station wagon with wooden panels. I tried to stay as far from them as I could. They got on the highway and were headed toward Indianapolis. They passed Deer Creek, turned onto highway 218 and went about two miles. They stopped at a graveyard, got out, each carrying a briefcase. Both girls went into the graveyard. They stopped at a tomb and looked around before going inside. I pulled over and put on the mechanic's suit I kept in the trunk. The back had *Landscaper* embroidered in dark green. I also had a gold standard make-up kit that would have made Red Skelton jealous. I put on a pair of glasses and walked to the nearby tool shed. It was open so I pulled out a rake and sauntered toward the crypt. The girls had been in there for at least fifteen minutes. Finally, half an hour later, they came out. I pretended to be raking, but they didn't even notice me, as they were very focused. Pam was carrying some sort of small machine and Sherry was carrying both briefcases. They put them in the car, got in, and sped off.

I went over to the crypt. It was an exact duplicate of the one in Logansport. The door was unlocked so I went in. I didn't see anything unusual. The only thing in it was one coffin that said Jimi Cryer, Sr. The date under it read August 1888 - June 1958. I looked around a bit more, but I didn't find anything. I had headed back to Logansport when I saw the girls' car parked behind a small cafe. I decided to pull in. They were sitting at a window booth and had just been served. I parked and went over to their station wagon. I popped the lock—station wagons were notoriously easy. I looked in the front seat and saw the machine Pam had been carrying. I picked it up to get a closer look at it. It was an odd-shaped machine, and I didn't see any way to turn it on. There were a few buttons but nothing worked. It was black, about six inches long and three inches wide, with three buttons. I was nervous about being caught, so I put the machine back and went to my car.

I waited a good twenty minutes for the girls to come out. I let them get ahead before pulling out after them. Half an hour later the girls were back at the house by the cemetery. I called it a day and went back to my room.

After I made a few calls, I found out that Bill's body still hadn't been found and neither had the two million. It didn't seem like I was making any headway. I had a reputation to preserve, after all.

The next morning I had just gotten dressed when there was a knock on the door. It was Nick. "Come in, Nick. No don't. Lets go have breakfast."

We went to the coffee shop and ordered coffee and pancakes. I told Nick the story of the cave. I then went on to describe the weird device I found in the girls' car. If that wasn't strange enough, I told him about Bill's missing body.

"I think Bill was ready to go into hiding long before getting picked up and put in jail," I said.

"I think you're right," Nick replied.

"The question is, who was he hiding from? Was he hoping the news of the missing two million would quiet down?" Nick asked.

"That would explain the radio we found in the cave," I remarked.

" I sure would like to see that cave sometime before it's turned over to the police." Nick remarked.

"We can do that." I said.

"Right now, Steve and I aren't sure we will ever turn it over to the police. Steve likes the idea of a place to go that no one knows about and so do I. Now that we have an easy access to the cave without getting wet, I might just see if the house is for sale. Of course, if I buy the house, you and Steve would always be welcome there," I said.

"I appreciate that, Joe, but I haven't even seen the

cave, yet. Maybe the three of us can go into this venture together," suggested Nick.

"That's possible," I said.

Steve must have heard us talking about him because he walked into the coffee shop, saw the two of us, and walked over to our table.

"Hi, Joe," Steve said,

"Hi Steve. Can you sit for a minute?"

"Sure. I'm off today." I introduced Steve to Nick, and after exchanging greetings, I explained our proposal for buying the house.

Thinking for a minute, Steve said, "Well, I do have an inheritance from my aunt in Chicago. What a swell lady she was. I was supposed to use it for college. But since I'm going into the Army, I won't be going to college. I'm in."

"You should still go to college," I remarked.

"I won't need it," he replied. "I'm going to be a helicopter pilot. The Army will train me."

"That's great," Nick and I remarked in unison. I asked who owned that old house. Steve said it belonged to an old farmer who was in a nursing home and had been for several years. "His name is

Howard Lipton."

"So you're a detective now?" I asked.

"No, but I couldn't get the cave off my mind," Steve said. "So I called and talked to him. He's willing to sell but wants to talk to us first."

The three of us went over to the nursing home in Nick's car. The home was huge and the yard was like a park. Residents were playing lawn games, reading or playing cards on the large front porch, or drinking what looked like iced tea in tall glasses. There were men and women in white uniforms milling about watching over them.

We stepped inside the lobby to the front desk. It looked very much like a hotel. Steve asked if we could see Howard Lipton.

"Why, yes," she said. "That's nice as he doesn't get any visitors. He's the last of the Liptons."

She took the three of us to a large room that was empty. *Activity Room* was spelled out above the door.

"I'll go get him." she replied. "Howard's room is a bit small for the three of you." Soon she was back with an elderly man and wheeled him up to the table.

Howard got out of the wheel chair. "I don't really

need it," he replied, "but they always insist."

I introduced everyone and went on to explain our interest in the house. I asked what his price was.

"First, before I give you my price, you need to know the story of that broken down old place," Howard said. "You see, I lived in that house all my life. I also own the property around it, about ten acres in all. My Dad grew tobacco there—one of the best places in Indiana to grow tobacco.

The government taxed us so much that it was no longer worth it to grow the tobacco. After my parents died, I tried growing other things like corn and potatoes, but the tobacco had taken most of the nutrients out of the ground. I was told it would be years before anything would grow there.

"So instead of farming, I decided to invest in emus, and that's where I made my fortune. There was a big farm not too far from mine, and that's where we kept them. I worked it every day for years until I ended up here. I sold my shares and now the farm will be all I have left to sell.

"Before we talk business, there are a lot of secrets you need to hear. It was more than my childhood home. It was a safe house for runaway slaves. There's a cave that runs through the basement where we used to hide them until it was safe to travel. And the biggest secret I can only tell to the new owners is..." Howard became quiet, like he was meditating.

"What's the secret?" I asked, wondering if he had drifted off.

"I can't tell you. You haven't bought my house yet."

"What's the price?" Nick asked.

"Thirty thousand dollars and no lower—the only and final offer.

"Let's go outside and talk it over," I suggested. We stepped outside the room and discussed the offer. We figured we could come up with ten thousand each for the purchase price, and then pitch in money and sweat to fix up the old house.

We went back into the room and told Mr. Lipton that we could meet his terms.

"Now can you finish your story, Mr. Lipton?" Steve asked.

"Not now," Howard said. "Not until I get my money and the lawyers finalize the deal."

"That could take weeks," I said, "How about if you call your attorney now and have him begin the process. I will give you a down payment of three thousand right now. "

While we waited, Howard talked to his lawyer on the phone. The lawyer then talked to each of us, getting our personal information. He said all we would have to do was come in and sign some paper work, bring in the balance of the money, and wait for the sale to close. Meanwhile, he would get Howard to sign off on the property.

"Now the secret," Steve said. Someone in a white coat brought in Howard's lunch.

"That does look good," Nick said. As they watched Howard eat, he began his story.

"When my great-grandfather bought that land, he discovered the cave by accident. He was digging out the basement for his new house by hand. The shovel slipped out of his hand, and it fell through the hole he was digging and disappeared. My great-grandfather realized that he had discovered a cave. After weeks of digging, he made the opening what it is today. He simply built the house around it. Except for the runaway slaves, no one else knew about the cave. But the real secret is..." And he hesitated.

"Come on." Steve said.

Howard took another bite of food, chewing slowly

and smiling at Steve. "Just kidding, young man. I knew I had your attention. As you know, there are several pockets in the lower part of the cave. But one has a secret door that my great-grandfather built.

"Behind that door is a labyrinth of tunnels that stretches for miles. They go in every direction, and they go very deep. They go as far as Logansport. One even goes to a cemetery. I don't know which one because my father would never tell me. And he wouldn't let me in the tunnels without him. I knew which pocket, but the door is made of a very heavy metal and I didn't know how to open it. Oh, as a young lad, I tried everything I could to open that door; I just never had any luck. And my dad died before he could tell me.

" A few years after my parents passed, I began going through all the things they had left. "That's when I found my dad's key to the big metal door in the cave. It was hidden, of all places, in a painting of the cave that my grandfather had painted.

"The painting was like one big jigsaw puzzle. It was a collage of scenes in the cave. One section of the painting was of the underground lake. In it were odd shaped stones and fish. A fisherman had a fishing pole in the water with a fish about to bite. The lure that the fish had latched on to was the key. My grandfather had actually carved a piece out of the painting so that the key fit right into it. Only upon careful inspection, could you tell that the key was removable.

"I thought that was so ingenious that I actually still keep the key in the painting. I still have them, and I'll give them to you as part of the sale if you promise never to sell it or take it from the house."

We all agreed in unison. "Where is the painting?" Joe asked.

"Oh it's still in the house. It's hanging in my grandfather's room, the first bedroom to the left as you go upstairs."

Mr. Lipton paused and looked at each of us in turn. I want each of you to remember one thing. When you open that metal door and start your journey, a strong sense of excitement will fall over you. It will be hard to think of anything else— and it will consume your life.

"You will see things not of this world. Things beyond you're comprehension. And there will be no turning back. Danger could lurk around every corner of the cave. My advice to you three is to just enjoy the cave and don't even think about the metal door or what's beyond it."

That's what my father and I did. He and I spent some

great times together exploring those tunnels. It's been a few years since I have been down there, but once, with my dad, we heard people talking. It was sort of an echo and they were saying the strangest things. You couldn't understand complete sentences, but there would be words like 'ready to transport,' or 'transport complete,' or 'Bentley in the oven,' or 'ready for blue diamond meltdown.' But we never could find anybody. And it didn't matter. We had a great time just being together. Heed my words, gentlemen."

It was just like we had heard on the radio. Nick and I looked at each other in astonishment. *A Bentley and a blue diamond were found in the Bronx.*

"Well, that's about it," Howard said. "I'm getting tired, boys. Steve, how was my story?"

"Riveting!" Steve replied.

"Well, its all true," Howard explained, "I think I will go to my room now, boys. I will have my attorney call you when the papers are ready."

CHAPTER NINE

We made plans to go to the cave again as soon as Steve could get his shifts covered. Nick and I wanted to spend a few days exploring, but insisted our new partner come along. That would give us time to get the money together for the lawyers and get any equipment we would need for the trip to the cave.

Nick decided go shopping for some warmer clothes. That cave would be cold. We all agreed and went shopping. We each bought long johns. Steve found a pair of earmuffs, remembering how cold his ears got in the tunnel. I bought walkie-talkies for the three of us. Nick bought three ropes, weatherproof matches, and three pairs of gloves. He started to buy flashlights, but I told him about the cases of flashlights stored in the cave.

The following day, I got a phone call from the lawyer informing us that Howard had passed away. He had revised his will so that the three of us were to get the house as a final gift. The rest of his estate would go to an animal rescue farm nearby. I was excited about the house but sad about Howard. The lawyer told me the funeral would be the following day and we were welcome to attend. Afterwards, we could sign the papers for the house.

It was a small funeral. The three of us were there, a few from the nursing home, and Howard's lawyer. It barely lasted an hour. We all went to the graveyard service, and I thought it was sad that there were no family members left to be there. After the funeral, we went to the lawyer's office to sign the papers.

The lawyer gave me my three thousand dollar check back along with the deed to the house, which was made out in all three names. It was a bittersweet moment for the three of us; we liked Howard and wished we could have gotten to know him better.

It was an understatement to say the house we had just inherited needed a lot of work. Nick and I decided we would move in and get started as soon as we could move out of our current homes.

We were coming up with questions that we never thought of before. If one of us got married would we continue to live there? Could we sell our share to a stranger? We needed to talk these things over, so we made some decisions and had Howard's lawyer write up a contract that was fair to all of us. Our main concern was that we didn't want strangers living in the house, so it was decided that we had first rights to buy one another out. We decided we could start working on the house the following day. Nick rented a van, which gave us more room for all of the equipment we would need. The next morning we were off and running.

After arriving at our house, Nick took one look and said loudly, "What did I get myself into?" The shingles were falling off, the gutters had deteriorated long ago, there was no paint left on the house, and the weeds had taken over. It was like the start of a scary novel.

When we went into the house, it got even worse. The boards were creaking with every step we took, the floor had no linoleum left, and there was even water in the globe dangling from the ceiling light.

Steve went upstairs and found three bedrooms and a bath. The upstairs didn't look as bad as the downstairs. He yelled down, "I've got dibs on the last bedroom."

"Ok," Nick and I yelled back. There were three rooms, a large pantry, and a decent sized laundry room. Nick was beginning to feel nauseous about how much money would be spent fixing the place up. We now understood the term *buyer's remorse*.

After a bit, we decided to take a break from the repairs and go down into the abyss. I led the way to the basement. Steve opened the door to the cave, flashlights in hand. At the end of the long tunnel, Nick found himself in a small room. As he shined his flashlight around the room, he saw a mechanical device in front of him. "What's that?" Nick asked.

"It's a lift that will lower us to the bottom," Steve answered. I thought it best if Steve lowered himself first. Then he could start the generator while we came down. Steve explained to us that he would have to lower himself slowly, pushing the lever forward because pulling back would put on the brakes.

Nick picked up a pebble and tossed it into the water below. There was a rippling effect shining off the water. That's when Nick decided he had made the right decision to invest in this house.

Soon the generator was purring. Nick remarked, looking down, that he hadn't ever seen anything so beautiful. Soon the three of us were in the main cave looking at the pockets in the wall.

I got into my duffel bag that I had brought with me and handed Nick and Steve each a helmet with hooks that would support a flashlight. Once the flashlights were hooked securely, we put them on. I had also brought each of them a backpack. They contained a small first aid kit, food rations for a day, and ropes tied to the back. "Who's the Boy Scout, now," I said smiling. Nick and Steve were impressed.

Nick looked at all the pockets in the wall—there must have been a hundred. We needed to get a closer look at them to find anything resembling a handle or lever that moved.

Steve suggested they each take a section of the cave. Nick took the east wall. I took the west, and Steve took south wall. The north wall, which was the opening from the lake, had no pockets.

I was moving from pocket to pocket, not finding anything. We skipped the pockets that were packed with the supplies that Bill had left. About an hour later, we were about done and still had not found the door.

"I wish we could have asked Howard which pocket it was," Nick said, frustrated.

With a smile on his face, Steve said, "Howard did tell us. He said it had a big metal door. Maybe we need to hammer on the rocks until one sounds like metal."

"Great idea," I said, wondering why I didn't think of

it an hour ago. Nick found an old rusted Army shovel that was folded. It took all of us prying to get the shovel open, rust falling to the cavern floor. One pocket at a time, we hammered on the walls. Fifteen minutes and three pockets down the south wall later, we heard a clang.

"We found it," I shouted excitedly. I tried pulling on the rocks but nothing happened. Puzzled, I put my hand on a rock, using it for leverage so I could climb higher. The rock moved sideways and I lost my balance, falling backwards. Nick and Steve moved forward to catch me.

Then something amazing happened. The rocks slid out of sight and there before us was a big metal door. It was brass in color and looked very thick. We then saw the keyhole.

"We don't have the key," I exclaimed. "I don't think we can pick that lock! And it isn't the same kind of key in Mr. Lipton's painting."

Nick looked closely at the lock and then turned to me excitedly.

"Joe, the satchel you showed me had a key. Do you have it with you?"

"I sure do," I said.

I pulled out the satchel, reached in, and pulled out the strange metal key.

"Who wants the honors?" I asked, holding out the key. With youthful exuberance, Steve grabbed it, put it in the lock and turned it. The door slid out of sight.

"Why don't we sit and take a lunch break before we enter the other cave," I suggested as my stomach rumbled. There were some meals in the boxes in the pocket. We would eat those and save the rations in our backpacks for later on when we were deeper in the tunnels. I found dried beef and crackers and Nick found some water. Ten minutes later, we were ready to go.

I said, "There are no lights beyond this door so we need to make sure we don't get separated." The three of us tied ourselves together.

"Wait," Nick said. "We need something to mark our way back."

"Way ahead of you," Steve said shaking a can of fluorescent spray paint. "I have two."

We were only two feet into the cave when I saw a bag that looked like an over-sized doctor bag. It was on a ledge to my right. I stopped and opened it. I couldn't believe it. It was the missing money.

"Well, another case solved," I said.

Steve and Nick looked in astonishment at the large pile of small bills.

"I have never seen so much money," Steve exclaimed. "Bill must have put the money there after the robbery."

"That means he knew about the door," I said. "Instead of hiding the money in the Erie Avenue house, he hid the key."

"Let's leave the money here for now," I said, "and finish our exploring." As we continued another mile in, the lights above ended. We turned on our headlamps, which was more then enough light. Steve suggested we just use one to save batteries. "We have plenty of batteries," Nick said. "I emptied some of the flashlights and brought extra."

"Good thinking," I said as I flipped my flashlight back on. The trail was headed downwards, maybe a quarter mile underground. *And still going deeper.* After about twenty minutes the cave got wider, about twenty feet on each side of us.

I could see soda straw stalactites hanging from the ceiling. Nick jumped up when he saw a snake slithering away. Steve laughed and said it was just a Black Rat Snake. "It's not poisonous," he said. There were lots of boulders lying around, so we untied ourselves and took a break using the boulders as seats.

When we got up, we headed forward in the cave, which began to narrow. Before long, we came to a section where several tunnels took off in different directions. I decided we should keep heading forward instead of turning so we wouldn't get lost. The other two agreed and Steve marked our way back with the spray can.

We found ourselves walking uphill, now, in another big opening twice the size of the previous one. There were huge stalagmites and stalactites all around. As we sat on a big boulder admiring the sight, I found myself getting sleepy. Nick was yawning and Steve was already asleep. I started to get up but I must have passed out. Nick, too, fell to the ground in a deep sleep.

When we woke up, we all had major headaches.

"What happened?" Steve asked.

"I don't know," I said. *It was like some sort of gas had been released.* We decided we should continue, so we went forward. The cave started getting smaller. We came to another metal door. I tried the same key and it worked.

Beyond the door was a ledge; we stood in amazement. About fifty feet below us were hundreds of people working on strange machines. Letters and pictures were coming from TV screens all around the room. Everyone was dressed in long, blue suits with gold stripes down the side. One of the machines was fairly large. A man sat on the seat in the back of it. A long rod came out of it like a cannon and a large TV screen was in front of him. There was an image of a blue Dodge Charger on the screen.

"Initiate," someone ordered. The man pulled a lever and the Dodge Charger appeared in front of their eyes.

More and more items were zapped into the room. It was so strange we thought we were hallucinating. *Maybe it was the gas.* I was too afraid to speak.

Then we heard a familiar voice. It was Pam. She was looking right at us. "We were expecting you. Come on down." More than a bit shaken, we went down. I noticed no one took their eyes off the TV screens. Pam told us to follow her and she would explain everything to us.

She took us into a room filled with more machines than I had never seen before. There was a large table with chairs. "Sit down," Pam offered.

"Are we in some sort of military facility?" I asked.

"Not quite," she shrugged. "We are from the future. Our goal is to learn from the past. We assist people whenever possible trying to make their lives better. However, there's only so much we can do. We can only help in small ways, but we cannot do anything directly that will change the future. For example, whenever you had a war we were there helping in small ways. Take the German Enigma Machine. We gave you Americans the clues to breaking the code.

We can't be everywhere, but we do what we can. Our business can be stressful, so for fun our hobby is to retrieve lost or stolen items and return them either to the owner or to the family. Sometimes we have to wait years. Often no family members are left, so we put them in odd places where they will do the most good—like the Bentley in the Bronx. But our main goal is to learn.

"Think of this place as a university. Tomorrow, I'm scheduled to watch Lincoln die at Ford's Theatre. The day after that, I'll watch George Washington cross the Delaware. We start early in life studying the past so we learn what we should and shouldn't do when it's our time. It is a delicate line between can do and should do. Only the best are allowed to participate in this "university." First, we must have an IQ of at least two hundred. Then it takes ten years of studying before we are allowed to go into the past."

When I asked her what Bill had to do with all of this, Pam responded that Bill went rogue. He fell in love, which is a big no-no. "He got married twenty-five years ago. Our High Commander warned Bill that his funding would be cut off, but Bill didn't care. He was too in love with his wife to give her up. It took us twenty-five years, but we found an opportunity to bring Bill back. We knew he had become a drinker. When we found out he had been arrested, we planted a man named Mark Binger in the jail. He gave Bill a drug that slowly made him look like he'd had a heart attack. The drug made it seem like Bill was dead, but he wasn't. We went to the funeral home, stole him back, and sent him back to his time, the future.

"All those items that showed up all at once?" she continued laughing, "We had a glitch in the system. We sent items back to thousands of people at once. It took us days to fix it."

"Who is Sherry?" I asked.

"Enough for today, guys. We have a room for the three of you. I'm afraid you will have to spend the night."

"What do you plan to do with us?" Steve asked. "Just talk," Pam said. "There isn't much more we can do without changing the future."

The room we were given was big and well furnished. We each had our own bed. Someone brought us a hot chicken dinner, complete with mashed potatoes, coleslaw, and biscuits. Boy, was it good. The food made us tired and soon we were asleep.

The next morning, we woke up feeling surprisingly good. Pam met us at the door. She gave us a tour of the facility and filled us in on the purpose of the strange looking machines.

"These machines are computers. Soon, in your lifetime, every one will be using them."

I showed Pam the picture of someone talking to himself. She laughed and said it was a cell phone. "You will have one of your own someday and will wonder how you ever got along without it." Then she took me to the object that looked like a roller coaster. She explained that is how all the workers get here. "They sit in the seats, set the date, time, and coordinates. Instantly they are transported to this facility. For a single person needing transportation, we have a smaller version."

"What about the machine that Sherry was carrying

in the graveyard by Deer Creek?" I asked.

"Oh, that was just a small device that can transport small objects like a baseball or a bicycle." She smiled remembering the little boy who lost his.

I had so many questions and wanted them all answered now. "And who are Sherry and Jimi?"

"Sherry's job is to interact with people and see how they differ from year to year and from culture to culture. Jimi is Head Commander. He gives us our assignments. We have been called back, so we are slowly moving out and will soon be gone along with all of our equipment. There will be no sign that any of us had ever been here. We have been called to a new location. Chances are that we will never meet again. So, if by chance we do, don't be upset if I pretend not to recognize you. Good bye, gentlemen."

The next thing we knew, we were back in the old basement of the house.

"No one will ever believe us," I whispered to myself. Nick held out his hand and we sealed the deal by shaking hands—we would not reveal our secret cave to anyone. "Now lets get busy cleaning our new home."

CHAPTER TEN

The following day I got hold of George Brill and Rex Hanson and handed them the two million. I told them to give Mrs. Cryer all of the reward money. I said I only wanted twenty thousand to fix up my new house.

"Yes, another case solved," I said with a smile of satisfaction. I reached into my coat pocket and took out the socket with the crystal on it. *I never did find out what this weird looking thing was for.*

Later that evening, Steve and Nick met me at the graveyard. We were going to go into the crypt. The door was unlocked so we went in. The room wasn't that large, so it was easy to search, but we still couldn't find anything unusual. No hidden room no hidden levers. Puzzled, Steve leaned against the coffin. It moved. There was a door on the floor with a weird shaped lock. I bent closer and realized the crystal socket looked like a perfect fit. It was. As soon as I fit it into the lock, the door popped open. There was a set of stairs going down to a room under the crypt.

Steve found a light switch and flipped it up. You can imagine our surprise to find gold bars, gold coins, ancient gold goblets, and diamonds. Three chests with our names on them sat next to the mounds of gold.

Pam, Sherry, and Jimi came out into the light.

"We didn't think it fair to leave without a goodbye. Each of you needs to open your chest."

I went first. "I don't believe it," I said. There was the Dick Tracy decoder ring I had lost long ago, the six-gun I played with as a kid, comic books, and lost pictures of my mother. My tears made it difficult to look at the pictures of Grandmother, Granddad, and Aunt Nelly.

Steve opened his next. He found the set of baseball cards he had lost as a kid, and the wallet he lost last year in a hayloft. The chest was full of lost items from his childhood.

Finally, Nick looked in his. There was a model car kit he never got to put together because his brother hid it on him and wouldn't tell him where it was. Old family photos filled his chest.

Pam explained all the gold had been unclaimed for hundreds of years, and said that we should put it to good use. Of course, we promised. With a hug, Pam, Sherry, and Jimi were off.

So the next time you watch the news and the top story is that a rare lost Rembrandt has been found, or your local paper headline reads: Jewish Gold and Jewels Returned to Rightful Heirs, you will remember my story.

ZORKO

Zorko was a businessman first and foremost. His kind did not become involved in the lives of the human book characters that he bought and sold. But somehow, Maggie was different. There was something about her that caught his interest more than the other book characters. He had been observing her for many years, and he needed her to be a complete set, as it would benefit him financially. He would become the most respected of booksellers.

The more he watched Maggie, the more he became involved in the complexity of her life, which meant more volumes. She needed to be complete. There were some things missing that would make this set the envy of all book owners. He knew it would take time, but he was determined to do it.

Maggie, he knew, was a capable

businesswoman. She kept meticulous records of everything from the running of the ranch to her Town Council meetings. Fortunately for him, she kept a daily journal. There weren't very many entries documenting her emotions (something we do not understand). At least there weren't until this Joe guy came into the picture.

Zorko finished Joe's first journal, but there was no mention of Maggie. He wondered when the two of them met and how important Joe really was to her. Does he belong in her book set? Zorko was thinking the High Commander would pay handsomely for a new volume to the set of Maggie.

Zorko prepared for a return trip to Earth. On the way, he would read more about this Joe Craig.

THE CAVE JOURNALS
PART TWO

CHAPTER ONE

It had been two years since I'd worked on a big case. I was been busy fixing up our house out in the country. As with all houses, there is more work than time. It was good having this break as my last case was difficult, to say the least. But the time came when it was necessary to get back to what I love—solving cases.

I got in the habit of journaling my days. I'm a pretty smart fella, but I found that, sometimes, I needed to step back from what was happening and revisit it at a later time. Putting details, feelings, and even questions on paper had come in handy more than once.

Steve was the first one to check out the upstairs, so he got dibs on the biggest bedroom. He had finally joined the Army and was in helicopter training. Before long, he will finish training and be a full-fledged pilot, which was what he wanted to do for most of his life. What he didn't know was that the house had been enlarged by almost half—most of it in my bedroom. I finally had a bed big enough to stretch out on, my own bathroom, walk-in closet, a couch, and my own outside entrance. I even put in my own elevator to the cave! I couldn't wait for Steve to see it all.

Nick was always busy. He spent a lot of time doing charity work. Helping out the local farmers is his thing. He helped most of them in one way or another—equipment, work hands, whatever they needed. The money left to us was being put to good use. No one else knew about it, so that allowed us to help anonymously. About every other week, Nick checked in on his hardware store, grateful that his manager was so capable. Nick also has an occasional customer that needs fake IDs. Just so no one gets the wrong impression about Nick, he only makes fake IDs for private investigators or someone on the police force needing to go undercover. He only makes them for people who have a legitimate excuse for needing a fake ID.

I got a call to work on a case involving a fugitive. I looked over the portfolio and it seemed a man named Boris used false documents from a judge to get out of prison. There had to be help from the outside, so I headed to Washington D.C. to talk with the officials in charge of this case.

When I arrived at the police station in D.C., the captain gave me all the information I needed. It seemed there was a Russian immigrant by the name of Boris Petrov who escaped custody. Boris had been in the United States for a year. He was supposed to go back to Russia after six weeks, but he robbed a liquor store and killed the owner. He was given life in prison, but escaped on the way to the pen. The authorities had not been able to catch him. Knowing my reputation for solving cases, they asked for me, Joe Craig.

CHAPTER TWO

The police captain mentioned that Boris had distant relatives living in a small Russian community just outside of Philadelphia, PA, so I decided to rent a car and drive there. It was a twelve-hour drive, so I decided to make a small road-trip out of it.

I arrived mid-day and had some good daylight left to do some investigation. After questioning some of the locals, I found the small community of Russians the captain had told me about. After showing Boris' picture around, I found out he had been there and had just robbed yet another liquor store. According to what witnesses told the police, it seemed he was now headed to Ohio. He was with a woman, but no one seemed to know her name. One man told me that when she opened the trunk of her car, he saw a brown box that said Dayton Hotel. That would be the best place to start, I figured.

"What kind of car?" I asked.

"It was an ugly green car," the man retorted. "Maybe a Chevy. I think the back left taillight was cracked."

"Do you know what year?" I asked.

"No, but that won't matter," the man replied. "You'll know the car when you see it."

So I set my sights on Dayton, glad that this rental car had unlimited mileage. It was late, but after a long day's drive, I found a cheap motel called Ducks Inn. It wasn't in the best of neighborhoods, so before checking in I made sure my .38 Special was loaded and ready for use. My room wasn't too bad. It could have used a little more cleaning, but I guess it's true: You get what you pay for. I slept in my clothes on top of the covers and used my jacket as a blanket. I was reasonably comfortable.

The next morning, I was ready to check out when, to my surprise, there was an ugly green Chevy in the parking space four doors down. I looked at the left taillight. Sure enough, it was cracked. I didn't know if I should go in with guns blazing, wait outside, or maybe call for backup. I decided on the latter. I'm no slouch; I'm pretty quick on my feet for my size, but these Russians can be pretty tough. Five minutes after my call, six—count them, six—police cars showed up. *Who was patrolling the rest of the city?* I explained to the officers that Boris Petrov was a fugitive from Washington D.C., and that I was a private investigator hired by the D.C. police to find him. I showed them his mug shot. The officer in charge wanted confirmation that it was Boris who was registered to that room. The desk clerk said no one by that name was registered, but a Miss Branson was. A man with Boris's description, however, was with her.

With their guns drawn, the officers approached the motel room. There was no response to their demands that he open the door. The police decided to evacuate the motel. I thought that was a little bit much, but who am I to tell the police what to do? After the motel was evacuated, they shot tear gas into Boris' room. Just then, the S.W.A.T. team arrived, big van and all. I just shook my head. *Why don't they call in the National Guard, as well? It's one man in a motel room.* By now I was regretting my decision to call in the police. The S.W.A.T. team rammed the door. Two others stormed the room, with a third bringing up the rear. It wasn't long before we heard the words, "Clear! All clear!" The swat team came out alone. *Funny. I didn't hear any shots.* The police went in and I followed.

"Don't touch anything," I heard. It was a Captain Jarred. There was a dead body on the bed; it was Miss Branson, the young woman that left town with

Boris in Philadelphia. A sheet covered her, but you could see by the position of the blood splatter that her throat had probably been cut. Her purse was dumped on the floor, but there was no wallet. *Boris must have taken it. He only scored a couple hundred from his last robbery so he must be short on cash.*

Captain Jarred ordered everyone out; C.S.I. was taking over. I saw them open their medical bags, take fingerprints, blood samples, and pictures. There wasn't any more I could do until they finished their work, so I followed Captain Jarred to the police station.

After ordering an APB for Boris Petrov, the Captain motioned for me to follow him into his office. "Why don't we go to lunch, Joe. No sense waiting here." I eagerly agreed, so we went to a local hamburger joint. He ordered the bacon burger, and I did the same.

We sat outside at a table close to his car discussing the case when we heard, "Car four. Calling car four. Captain are you there?"

Captain Jarred went to his car. "This is car four. Come in," he said.

A voice suddenly came from the speaker inside his car, "Someone fitting the description of Boris Petrov just robbed a liquor store on Hwy. 8. He was last seen in a white Ford Falcon heading in the direction of Connecticut. Witnesses failed to get a description of the plates, but they said the Falcon is a newer model with a *Go Red Socks!* sticker on the back bumper." The captain and I headed back to the police station, and I told him I would call later to see if he had any more information on Boris.

I headed to Hwy. 8. *I miss my Camaro.* This rental car was more of a town car. Note to myself: rent a faster car.

CHAPTER THREE

I drove all evening and through the night. I saw a **Rest Stop One Mile** sign up ahead. The time was five a.m. Two hours sleep would do me. That way, I could get back on the road by seven. I pulled into the rest area and saw a few cars, a couple of trucks, but no white Ford Falcon, so I closed my eyes and slept.

I woke up to the sound of a tractor-trailer pulling in. I looked at my watch, and saw that it was nine a.m. I really must have been tired. I hurried to the restroom and splashed cold water on my face. I needed to wake up and get going. I was way behind schedule. Boris already had a good head start on me. As I pulled out onto the highway, I couldn't believe my luck. The first car I saw was a white Ford Falcon and it had that same bumper sticker. Boris must have stopped even earlier than I did.

I was used to tailing people so I stayed behind Boris for several miles. Unfortunately, the gas light came on. I had to do something quickly, so I pulled up close to the Falcon to make sure it was Boris. I looked closely at the man inside; it was Boris. He looked back at me and I knew I had been made, I couldn't lose him, and so I rammed my rental car into the right side of his car. Boris swerved, but easily regained control. He knew just by looking at me that I was intent on stopping him. Boris struck back with a vengeance. When he was almost behind me, he swerved his Falcon toward the backside of my car, forcing me into a tailspin. My car hit the side rails on the highway, sputtered, and then died. I must have blacked out for a few seconds because I woke up to see Boris speeding away. I tried in vain to start the car, but it was hopeless. A man stopped to help me, but when we failed to get the car running, he drove me into the nearest town, Minesport.

I headed to the police station. I told the officer, Jack Turner, all about Boris and why I was on his tail. Once he had finished his report and confirmed my story, he put out an updated all points bulletin on the Ford Falcon. He then put down his pen and looked at me seriously. He gave me a lecture about how dangerous and foolish I was. I would be lucky if I didn't get arrested myself. He told me not to leave town, but I insisted I needed to catch up to Boris. He told me I had a choice—get a hotel room or a jail cell. I chose the hotel room.

"By the way," I said, speaking to the cop. "Boris's specialty is robbing liquor stores. If he's short on cash, that's where he'll head." The cop gave me the thumbs up, as if to say he understood me. I headed out to find a place to spend the night.

Finding a hotel was easy; there was one right across the street from the police station. I registered and was give keys to room 222. I opened the door and saw a fake fireplace surrounded by cheap pictures. There was a double bed, an end table, and a small desk. The first thing I did was to take a shower to wash off the events of the day. And, as usual, I found myself struggling to hang on to those small soaps that come with the room. After my shower, I decided to take a quick nap before renting another car. Six hours later, a knock at the door awakened me. I looked at the clock. *So much for a quick nap.*

"Who is it?" I asked groggily.

"It's Jack—Officer Turner. I have some news for you." I got up slowly and answered the door. "Come on in," I said sitting back down on the bed. Jack sat down in a chair next to the bed.

"Have a seat," I offered sarcastically. Grinning, Jack told me the State Police found the white Ford Falcon that Boris had been driving. He also said that someone had used a credit card belonging to Miss Branson. They withdrew two hundred dollars, the daily maximum she was allowed.

Then Jack added, "The money was withdrawn in Water Boy, Connecticut." He said that the State Police were keeping all of her credit cards active. That way they can keep tabs on Boris' whereabouts. "That's good," I told Jack, appreciating his update. "Are you charging me with anything?"

"No, but I should," Jack said slowly. "The townspeople don't want to feed you."

I gave him a sarcastic look and asked if he knew where I could rent a car. "Nowhere until morning," Jack said. "Everything is closed. After your accident with the last rental, good luck trying to get another." He stood up. "Well, I'm going to call it a night." He nodded his head and headed out the door.

I wasn't tired, so I decided to watch TV for a while, but I fell asleep. A few hours later, I woke up to the sound of a rooster crowing and white snow on the TV. I had to laugh. This must be a small town.

Looking at my watch, I saw it was already after six. I got dressed and hoped I could find a restaurant open this early. I checked myself in the mirror and ran the comb through my dark black hair. Satisfied, I left my room. I walked outside the hotel and up and down the street. I couldn't find a restaurant open, even though I passed two.

A police car pulled up. It was Jack. "Hunting for somewhere to rent a car?" Jack asked me.

"No," I replied. "I'm really hungry."

"You should have looked in the hotel," Jack said. "The coffee shop opens at five."

"Guess that makes me the dummy," I grinned. It never crossed my mind to check the hotel.

"That's where I'm headed," Jack said. By the time he had parked the police cruiser, I had caught up with him. I was surprised at how many people were in here at this time of the morning.

The waitress came over to our booth, "Coffee, guys?"

"Yes, please," I said sounding a bit desperate. The waitress poured us each a cup, and then took our order. I ordered the Mexican omelet with hash browns and sourdough toast. Jack just had two over-hard eggs with English muffins.

"And throw some cheese on those eggs," Jack added as the waitress was leaving.

Jack said that there wasn't any further progress in the search for Boris.

"As soon as I get a car, I'm going to head over to Water Boy," I said to Jack. "Maybe I can do some snooping around. What do people in a small town like this do, anyway?" I asked.

"Mostly farming," Jack answered. "We also have a paper mill that employs about fifty people. That's about it. It's a quiet town, but we do have a lot of tourists driving through. They spend a little money here. It helps keep people employed. Gas, car repairs, restaurants—all helps keep the economy going."

"And you can't forget speeding tickets." I chuckled at Jack's last remark.

"And where around here can I rent a car?" I asked again.

"As I said earlier, nowhere here. We don't have a car rental in Minesport. The nearest one is a good fifty miles away. However," he added with a grin, "there are a lot of good working cars here for sale. Billy, about four blocks from here, has a nice 1964 Mustang for sale. He got it cheap and spent all his hard earned money fixing it up. There's a "For Sale" sign on the car now. Runs like brand new, probably better. Billy may be young, but boy is he a good mechanic. I can give him a call if you want," Jack suggested.

"No, just give me directions," I replied, thinking I didn't want Billy to know ahead of time that I was desperate for a vehicle. We finished breakfast, and I went back to my hotel room, packed my suitcase, and looked around to make sure I didn't leave anything behind. I used up the last of my cash to pay my hotel bill, so I decided to find a bank before heading to Billy's.

Only a few minutes into my errand, I tripped over a buckled sidewalk and immediately fell to the ground. It must have been obvious that I was struggling to get up, because a passerby stopped to help. After thanking the man and getting over my initial embarrassment, I limped across the street to a park with empty benches. I needed to get off this foot for a few minutes.

I was taking off my shoe when I saw, of all people, Pam and Sherry walking toward me. I was excited to see them, as it had been two years since we last talked. I explained to them how I tripped on the sidewalk and sprained my foot—and that I was just resting it for a bit.

"We know," Sherry said with raised eyebrows and

that *have-you-forgotten-who-we-are* look. I was puzzled and looked at them questioningly. Then Pam reminded me that they were from the future.

Sherry added, "We knew you would be at this park bench at this exact moment. We're here to give you something, Joe," Pam said. Then Sherry handed me three coins, each on a chain. They were silver in color, and had *The Truth* stamped on them. Pam instructed me not to lose them or give them up, as there could be disastrous consequences. I was to give one to Nick and one to Steve when I saw them next. Pam went on to explain that the coins were made of a metal not found on earth and that they would glow a bright gold color whenever I saw the truth.

My foot was now throbbing and I bent again to take off my shoe. When I looked back up to thank the girls, they were gone. Pam and Sherry had just vanished. As strange as I thought this to be, what seemed stranger, were their words, "whenever I saw the truth." I had no idea what that meant.

I continued to sit on the bench for nearly an hour just watching people go by. I wasn't sure what had just happened and what connection it had to the case I was working on. A guy trying to steal an elderly woman's purse brought me back to the present. Before I could react, she beat him with her umbrella. She was beating the thief so hard that he started screaming for help. I rather enjoyed the scene, but eventually the would-be thief found his chance and got away. As I continued to rest my foot, I also watched the activity around me—people throwing Frisbees to their dogs, others throwing crumbs to the birds, and squirrels gathering nuts falling from the trees. It was a peaceful, yet familiar scene. This could be any city anywhere.

The pain in my foot finally started to subside. I thought I could walk well enough to make it okay to the bank and then on to Billy's place. I found the bank just down the block, went in and withdrew $5,000. Now it was time to see that Mustang.

CHAPTER FOUR

Billy was outside washing the car when I got there. I introduced myself and explained to him that I was interested in this rebuilt Mustang of his. I really liked the long hood and short deck of the Mustang.

"What's under the hood?" I asked trying not to sound *too* interested. I could tell Billy was proud of this car by the way he responded.

"A v-8. It should produce 271 horsepower."

"Nice pony car," I said making a slow circle around it. "Can I take it out for a spin?" I asked Billy.

"Only if you're a serious buyer," Billy said. "I can't afford the gas."

I offered to give him something for the gas if I didn't buy the car. Billy agreed, so I got behind the wheel and Billy climbed in beside me. I put the car through some quick maneuvers with Billy hanging on for dear life. Once we were back at his place, I told him what a great car the Mustang was, and that he had done a fantastic job restoring it.

It was worth every penny, so I handed $3,000 over to Billy. Beaming, he thanked me and handed me the title. I was thrilled to be driving such a swell car once again.

As I pocketed the paperwork, I fingered the necklaces Pam and Sherry had given me. I pulled one out and clumsily put it around my neck. I put the car in gear and turned to wave goodbye to the young mechanic. Suddenly, my blood ran cold and I slammed on the brakes. Billy's face was like that of a monster. The sides of his forehead were shrunken in and there were holes where his ears should have been. The holes were filled with worm-like tentacles that writhed in slow motion, in Medusa fashion, as if in response to an unearthly tune. His large nose was more of a snout and his lipless mouth was just a large, dark hole in the center of his face. The scariest part was his eyes. The piercing black orbs felt as though they were looking right through me clear to my very soul. He had long, thick, black, fingernails hanging from arms that were fuzzier then a hippy auditioning for a part in *Hair*. His dull, clay red body seemed menacing as he lurched toward the car.

Frightened, I looked away and yanked off the necklace. I glanced back in the rear view mirror to see that it was once again just Billy. I was trembling worse then a San Francisco earthquake, but I managed to act normal and wave back. I stepped fast and hard on the gas pedal, leaving enough rubber to make two small ducks.

CHAPTER FIVE

Even though the trip to Connecticut went fairly fast, I barely remember the drive. I was still shocked by the transformation of Billy into that horrible monster. It took me a while to get my thoughts together; too many things had happened at once. Boris killed that poor woman, Pam and Sherry showed up with the necklace, and then I saw Billy in his true form. I thought I had seen everything. I wasn't sure how I could put all that aside to focus on Boris. I wondered what twisted thoughts were going through *his* mind—another robbery or was he going to hide out until things cooled down? Either way, I had to get my mind off Billy and on to finding Boris.

On a lighter note, even with the heavy rain and light fog rolling in, my new Mustang held the ground and ran great. I have always been a Camaro fan, but this car was making me rethink that. Both cars were an exhilarating drive.

Sooner than I expected, I arrived at Water Boy. As I drove around, I saw many nice motels, but I was holding out for the chance of finding a nicer hotel near the water. Hotels were like having your bologna sandwich with all the trimmings—lettuce, onions, tomatoes, and cheese. Motels were like eating just the bologna between two pieces of dry bread.

Finally, I found a great hotel with underground parking. I saw there were several security guards patrolling the area. I wondered how much that would cost me on my hotel bill. But I didn't mind. At least my new Mustang would be safe. Speaking of being safe, I put on my necklace. You never knew. I grabbed my suitcase and headed up the stairs to the front desk. Newspapers greeted me as I walked into the lobby. Papers from nine cities: New York. Chicago, Boston...it was like trying to figure out what kind of candy to buy in a candy store. All the headlines were pretty much the same— *Escaped Convict Still on the Loose*. Boris' picture was plastered all over the front pages, which might make him go deeper underground—and my job more difficult. I picked up the *Chicago Tribune* and headed to the front desk to register. The desk clerk, whose nametag identified him as Leonard, asked if he could be of service. I told him, that I wanted a room but that I didn't know for how long. He handed me a key, but before I went upstairs, I checked to make sure there was a coffee shop and bar on site.

My room key said 1004. I entered the elevator and started to push the tenth floor button when the closing door suddenly opened wide. I saw a monster following me onto the elevator. My heart began beating hard, but I tried to stay calm. The monster saw my necklace and snarled menacingly, "You! You have our necklace."

"What do you mean?" I asked, trying to steady my voice.

"You can see us. That's how we identify one another when we're in human form." With no hesitation the monster attacked me. He threw a right hook, and then hit me with a right punch to the jaw. I saw a left hook heading my way. I blocked it and came back with a kick to the monsters groin. I grabbed him by the head and smashed him into the side of the elevator wall. He squealed and pulled a six-inch jagged knife from his pocket. While the monster held the knife above his head, I grabbed his arm, and slammed his hand against my knee. I quickly pulled out my .38 Special and fired two shots into the monsters chest. The shots echoed loudly against the small elevator walls. After an anguished cry, he fell to the floor, dropping his knife. I stopped the elevator between floors knowing I was the only one that could see the dead man as a monster. I needed a moment to think what my next move was going to be.

I didn't need the police involved. How could I explain the dead man to them? The only way the police would believe my story was if I showed them how my necklace worked. And then, how would I explain how I got it in the first place?

The questions just kept on coming, and I slid to the elevator floor next to the dead monster. As my thoughts began to clear, I heard a voice come over the elevator speaker. The voice wanted to know what my problem was. Did I need any medical help? Was the elevator stuck? Before I could come up with a suitable answer, the monster disintegrated into a puff of smoke. The only thing left of him was a small pile of ashes. I didn't know what to think about the monster just disappearing like that, but it sure solved a lot of my problems.

I pressed the button next to the speaker, and let whomever was on the other side know that I was fine. Seriously shaken, I continued on to my hotel floor. I had experienced many strange things in my job, but these last few days were unbelievable. I finally made it to my room. I collapsed on my bed, but kept my eyes wide open. I still didn't have any leads to finding Boris, and if these monsters continued showing up, I never would find that guy.

I decided I would stay in for the night and planned to canvas the lower-income side of town tomorrow. The slum area was generally a good hiding place for criminals trying to lay low. There were fewer police patrolling the poorer areas, and the residents there were less inclined to talk about what was going on. It was sad but true.

At about midnight, I woke up in a cold sweat, shooting straight up from my bed. I just had the second nightmare of my entire life. I was in a graveyard with hundreds of monsters slowly walking toward me. I blamed this one on Pam and Sherry. My first nightmare occurred when I was seven. I had been at a Halloween party held at a haunted house. Witches and ghosts chased me throughout the house and there was nowhere to hide. It took until Thanksgiving before I could finally sleep without nightmares. I sure hoped it wouldn't take that long this time.

I knew sleep wouldn't come again, so I decided to get dressed and go to the bar. I chose the stairs. I didn't want to ride that elevator ever again—especially in the middle of the night!

I sat at the quiet end of the bar and ordered a bourbon and coke. I was hoping I could clear my mind of the monster and concentrate on my agenda tomorrow. Someone was playing soft music on the piano, which I greatly appreciated. My head wouldn't take anything loud at the moment. As I began to relax, my mind emptied itself of the trauma of the day.

After about three drinks, a young man came into the bar and sat next to me. He introduced himself as Wally. He was about six feet tall and on the handsome side. He had that rugged look that girls seemed to like—they must because girl after girl kept coming over to the bar to talk to him.

Wally told me he was a full-time student at the University. After getting to know him a little bit, I told him that I was a PI, and that I was in town to find a wanted man.

Wally told me he was a part-time guide, and if I needed a tour of the city, he was the guy. He then gave me his business card, which had his last name and phone number. I assured him that if I needed his assistance finding my way around town, I would definitely call him.

The next morning I woke up with a splitting headache. *How much did I drink last night?* I only remembered the first one. I went to the coffee shop, got some coffee, and bought some aspirin.

I spent the rest of the day checking out various areas of town and showing Boris' picture to anyone that would stop. I didn't seem to have any luck on my own so I decided to give Wally a call.

Maybe he could show me where certain ethnic groups hung out.

The next morning I met Wally in the lobby. He was wearing dark khaki pants and a light colored shirt. He was sure he could help me find the right area— he was up on the local neighborhoods because cultural diversity was part of his studies. Wally's words not mine. First, he took me by some bars where the Russians often hung out, but no luck finding Boris there. Next, we went to a Russian neighborhood. I showed the picture of Boris to at least a dozen people. Still no luck. We continued this long, boring routine all through the week. I wasn't sure how much more of this I could take. It was futile and expensive! I was ready to get out of Water Boy for good.

Wally and I managed to canvas pretty much the entire town in ten days. No one had seen Boris, or at least no one was talking. I figured I would pack my bags and head back home. I hated defeat.

As I finished up my packing, I half listened to the news. I heard a reference to two Russians. I looked up to see an amateur video of a fight between two men. It was two Russian men fighting in a tobacco field. Supposedly, the argument had started the night before. The video captured the bigger man killing the smaller one. And the bigger Russian was Boris, who took off with a stolen tobacco truck. The video had been recorded about six hours earlier. The newscaster stated that the truck was found on the outskirts of New York City. This was my first break in weeks, so I immediately changed my plans. Instead of going home, I headed to New York City.

CHAPTER SIX

By the next evening, I was on the outskirts of New York City. My gas light had just come on, so I stopped for gas. I stepped inside to pay, and as I was standing in line, I saw a rack with all kinds of maps. I picked up one of the city. It was just what I needed. It not only showed all of New York City's streets, but it also had a listing of local restaurants and hotels.

I returned to my car and checked the map to see where my current location was. As I studied the map, I heard two men talking. I glanced in the rear view mirror and felt fear creep over me. One of the men looked just like the monster version of Billy. I glanced down at my chest and pulled the necklace out from under my shirt. The coin glowed an eerie gold color. I quickly took it off and both men were once again normal looking. When I put the necklace back on, the one man was a monster again. I couldn't get out of there fast enough.

Was that what Pam and Sherry meant? By wearing the necklace, I would see that there are monsters amongst us? I was sure that was what they were trying to tell me. Then I wondered why they couldn't have just told me about the monsters. But I guess it's true: "Seeing is believing!"

I was more than a little nervous about seeing these monsters. They must not have seen my necklace because they left without so much as even a glance in my direction. I would have a hard time finding Boris if I had to keep fighting off monsters.

I forced myself to return to the map and found a place called the Chimney Hotel about two miles up the road. I thought I had better leave before more of these creatures showed up.

I checked into the hotel, and once I got settled, I pulled out the map and made my plans. As I fingered the necklace still around my neck, my mind jumped back to the monsters I had just seen. I didn't like seeing these creatures, but I also didn't like wondering if everyone I met was one of them. I was afraid my search for Boris would become secondary to fighting off monsters. What did these girls get me into and why?

It appeared to be about half an hour's drive to the waterfront. That was my starting point for tomorrow's hunt for Boris. Since his face was plastered all over the news, I was sure he would be searching for a more underground method of escape. Maybe he would hop a freighter since he spent so much of his time near the water.

The following day, I drove out to the carnival on the waterfront along the Atlantic. It was a beautiful day and the carnival was packed with people. No one had seen Boris, so I decided to quit for the day and head back to the hotel.

After a good night's sleep, I returned to the waterfront, again hoping for better luck. I was sure that was where Boris would hang out. People kind of kept to their old habits.

This time I went to another carnival at the far end of the waterfront. One of the employees at the Big Rides Carnival told me he had seen Boris. He was headed to Maine. "Yes, he was one lucky s.o.b. The fella that was supposed to work just quit, and this Boris fella showed up just at the right time. He and Pete left yesterday morning to pick up another new ride. They're in a semi-truck that had Big Rides Carnival written on the side of it."

I was in a hurry and decided to take a shortcut

through the back of the carnival. I had just passed an out-of-service ferris wheel when two men jumped me. Before I could see their faces, they put a black bag over my head. I was hit with some kind of metal object and knocked unconscious. I woke up to find myself tied to a metal hospital bed. I looked around and could see this really wasn't a hospital but rather an old abandoned building. Broken windows and old wooden cattle gates surrounded me. This place looked like it was from the Thomas Edison days.

I tried to wriggle free, but the leather straps were just too tight. I saw a monster not three inches away from me with a pair of pliers in his hand. He looked at me the way a cobra would just before it struck. He asked me where I had gotten the necklace. Now I was in a very disturbed mood. I answered back with, "from your mother." The monster, not saying a word, gestured for the other monster to come over. He held my mouth open while the other monster reached into my mouth with the pliers. He twisted the pliers back and forth until he pulled out one of my molars. Blood was squirting everywhere—on my face, on the monster, and on the bed sheets. I screamed in pain so loud that anyone within hearing distance would fear the building was going to collapse from the vibration.

I must have passed out because I woke up with my

mouth throbbing; the pain was unbearable. The monster holding the pliers was undeterred. Once again he asked me where I got the necklace.

Before I could answer with another smart remark, a young monster came into the room. He looked at me and then at the other two monsters. He then told them the High Commander wanted to see them and that he was to watch me. The young monster's voice sounded familiar to me. He told me he was Billy, the kid I bought my car from. I tried to pull myself together enough to respond. I asked him why he was here so far away from home.

Billy explained the High Commander had initiated him into the Royal Fleet of space ships because he had just turned eighteen. That was the law on Sagitar. Once a child turned eighteen, they became the property of the High Commander and were sent into whatever "service" the Commander ordered. Billy explained that his parents liked living on earth and didn't want to go back to their home planet. He also said he hadn't wanted to be initiated because he liked living on earth, too. He said he just wanted to go back home to Minesport, but if he didn't go through with his service, he and his whole family would be considered traitors. And not only would he be killed, but his parents and all other living relatives on his home planet would die as well.

I said that seemed a little extreme, and that if he would untie me, I would help him get back to Minesport. I would find a safe place for him and his family to hide, but I would not be able to help his relatives living on the home planet.

Billy said he would like to help me, but he couldn't take the chance. Before I could say anything further, the two monsters came back in. One monster took off a tool belt which held a gun and some other weird looking tools. He reached into the tool belt and again pulled out his pliers. The monster was headed toward me when Billy grabbed the gun from the toolbox and pulled the trigger. A long, red streak of light emerged from the gun and killed the monster. The other monster pulled his weapon and aimed it at Billy. Both fired at the same time and fell to the floor. Billy slowly crawled toward me, unable to get up. He reached his hands toward me with all the strength he could muster and unfastened the straps binding me to the bed. After freeing me, Billy collapsed and died in front of my eyes.

I looked down at Billy's lifeless body. Part of me was relieved that one more monster was gone, but the other part of me was saddened at the loss of such a young life. I worked rapidly to free myself and get out of there. Suddenly, I heard a poof sound. I turned quickly and saw all three bodies disappear in rapid succession.

I wondered if Billy had been born on Earth, or maybe even on the way to Earth. And had he ever seen his home planet Sagitar? Maybe Earth was the only home he knew. I guessed it didn't matter now.

I didn't know if any more monsters were behind the door, so I crawled out a window. Then I slid down a rusty old downspout. It held me for a moment before it gave way and plunged me down two stories.

Luckily for me I fell on a pile of hay in an old Chevy truck that was parked under the window from which I had just fallen. The truck was rusted out from years of sitting outside. I could tell that the truck had been used to haul hay to feed cattle. Pitchforks lay inches from where I landed. I knew I had to get out of here—and fast.

I ran as quickly as I could, considering what I had just been through. I saw a phone booth and called a taxi. It took a while for it to come, and I nervously watched in all directions in case another monster showed up. The pain in my mouth was unbearable, so the cabbie stopped at the drugstore so I could get something for the pain. The pharmacist showed me the strongest over-the-counter pain pills. I must have looked pretty ragged because he cautioned me about taking alcohol with them.

CHAPTER SEVEN

I quickly checked out of my hotel room and headed to Maine. I mapped out a new route of back roads that saved me a good hundred miles.

I drove for several hours before I finally saw a WELCOME TO MASSACHUSETTES sign. It was getting dark so I turned on my lights and radio. It was a quiet ride except for the soft music that was playing. My throbbing mouth seemed to be keeping time to the beat of the music.

Straight ahead I saw lights. Oddly, these lights were not on the road but in the sky. *Helicopter?* It seemed to be getting closer. I made out what seemed to be a hundred small lights. They were red in color, but about every fifth one had a bluish hue. I also saw a dome above the lights. *Whatever this thing was, it was big and I mean gigantic*! I guessed it was two city-blocks long. I suddenly realized it was some kind of space ship. *Is this where the monsters came from? Or is it one of those government experiments we hear about?* Whatever it was, it hovered right above me— maybe two hundred feet. Suddenly, my car died. This wasn't a good time for car trouble. I tried several times to restart it, but no luck. A bright light shone down from the spaceship into the woods not far from me.

I was directly under this enormous ship, and all I saw was its belly. Two tiny ships shot out from the underbelly of what I considered the mother ship. The tiny ships followed the light into the woods. Twenty minutes later, three tiny ships came shooting out of the woods and headed back to the mother ship. As soon as they were back in, I saw a flash of light, and the low-flying mother ship was gone. I guessed they must have been on a rescue mission since two ships went into the woods and three came out.

For some reason, I didn't think the spaceships scared me as much as watching Billie die. I was wrong, though, because I was actually shaking so bad I couldn't even drive.

All of a sudden, I saw a burst of light shoot from the sky. Then a bunch of small lights all headed toward me. The tiny spaceships arranged themselves in a circle and shot death rays directly at me. I jumped out of the car and ran toward the woods. They barely missed me and I found myself in knee-high, dead grass. The grass stretched for a few hundred yards before ending at the woods. The death rays caught the grass all around me on fire. I was in a real predicament. The fire singed my pant legs, and I had trouble seeing the woods through all the smoke. As I contemplated my next move, I saw a semi-truck come into view, and the tiny space ships diverted their attention to it.

All the tiny space ships aimed their weapons at the semi, their death rays blowing it into tiny fragments. I watched a tire roll across the road and realized it was the only thing that remained of the semi.

I saw my chance and ran into the woods and hid behind a tree. I watched the space ships as they headed my way. The tiny ships kept circling the woods, but didn't go into them. I guess one rescue mission was enough for them. They continued circling for another thirty minutes. Finally, they gave up and return to the mother ship.

I waited for a while, wondering why they didn't blow up my car. Maybe they wanted to catch me on the road again. Crouching low to the ground just in case the space ships came back, I headed toward my car. I didn't stop to think; I just needed to act. I turned the ignition key twice and, luckily, my Mustang began to purr.

I kept driving— I wasn't taking any chances. I did keep looking up in the sky, though, to make sure there were no signs of a spaceship. It wasn't like I could hear it coming. Soon I saw a small town ahead. Luckily there was a motel right off the road with a sign that assured me there were rooms available. As I reached the safety of the parking lot, my thoughts went to the driver of the semi, and I felt bad that his misfortune was what saved my life.

I sat in my car for a few moments, finally allowing myself to react. I was shaken to the core and couldn't shake the feeling that this all was far from over.

Once I checked into the motel and took a much-needed shower and went to bed. I must have been asleep for about six hours when the sound of someone in my room woke me up.

I acted like I was asleep, but at the same time I needed to see who it was. I was almost positive it was the manager of the motel. He was rifling through my wallet that I had left on the dresser.

When he turned his back to me, I jumped out of bed and tackled him to the floor. You can imagine my surprise when I saw that it was a young woman dressed as a man. She started screaming and clawing at my face. Not wanting to deal with her assault in the wee hours of the morning, I punched her in the mouth.

I must have hit her just right because she passed out. While she was unconscious, I tied her hands with my belt and then got dressed. As soon as she was awake, I said, "If you scream, I will punch you again."

She rubbed her bound hands over her now swollen lips and looked at me like I was the guilty one. In a low voice, she said that she needed bus money to escape the aliens that had captured her. I could tell by the look on her face that she was struggling to tell me her story—who would ever believe an alien abduction story was true?

"I was put in a spaceship and tied to some machine. When the aliens left the room, I slipped out of my bindings. I wandered around the spaceship going through different rooms trying to figure out how I could get out of there. Whenever I saw an alien, I hid behind one of the strange machines that were in all of the rooms. I finally saw the door to the spaceship was still open and slid down the hatch. I had to leave my purse behind. I escaped with nothing.

"Once on the ground," she continued, "I followed the road here. I'm really sorry, but I don't know what to do. My name is Becky and I really need your help. I promise you, I am not crazy."

I looked at Becky as she started to cry. I knew the feeling. I wished I could cry and get it all over with.

"How did you get those men's clothes?" I asked.

"I always dress this way," Becky shrugged. "Whenever I'm traveling, people think I'm a man, so they tend to leave me alone.

"My car is in the space ship somewhere. They just zapped it up along with me. I could see the space ship coming at me but I just froze."

"Where do you need to go, Becky?" I asked.

Before she could answer, two monsters came busting through the door. One grabbed Becky while the other came at me. My adrenaline was already high from my encounter with Becky. I dove for my .38 which was on the bed under my pillow. I grabbed it and got off three shots in rapid succession. One down.

I could see the other monster holding Becky, but I didn't dare shoot; I was afraid I would hit her. He dragged her out the door and into the parking lot. The next thing I knew, the monster and Becky were beamed up into the mother ship, which was right overhead.

I could see a large crowd had gathered outside,

staring into the dark sky above. The people were in awe of the space ship that covered half of their town. For some reason, no one was frightened; they simply stared. As they watched, the space ship slowly rose higher into the sky. As quickly and quietly as it had come, it was gone.

I was sorry that I failed to help Becky and hoped that somehow she would be able to escape again. I wondered how the monsters knew she was here in my room. *Had she been implanted with some kind of tracking device? Had she not known?* I didn't seem to have any answers.

CHAPTER EIGHT

I went inside my hotel room as the crowd began to dwindle. The next thing I knew, the State Police knocked at my door. It seemed they were taking statements from all of the witnesses.

The monster in my room had already disintegrated. I knew the police couldn't help Becky, so I left her and the monsters out of my statement, telling them pretty much the same story everyone else did. The police seemed satisfied with my statement; at least they didn't tell me to not leave town!

I had just gotten back to bed when there was another knock on my door. "Go away!" I yelled, exasperated and not in the mood for any more questions. The knocking continued, so I yanked open the door ready to take someone's head off.

"Hi, I'm Drake from the Sunday Times. Could I ask you a few questions about the spaceship?"

"No!" I retorted in the firmest voice I could find at this ungodly hour.

Drake shifted his body so that I couldn't close the door on him. *Smooth move. I would have to remember that one.* It was obvious that he wasn't going to give up easily, so I figured I would answer a few questions just so he would leave.

"Ok, Drake, you have five minutes—starting two minutes ago," I said firmly. He asked several questions that I knew he must have asked the others outside. "How big was the spaceship?"

"About half as big as the town," I replied.

"What else can you tell me about its appearance? Shape, color, lights?"

As I started to tell him what I remembered, I heard one of the state policemen say there would be a news conference in five minutes. Drake apologized and hurried out the door. *Thank you, State Police!*

I figured getting any more sleep was out of the question, so I got dressed once again. I packed my bags and headed toward the main office to pay my bill. The manager wasn't in the office. I had seen him at the news conference along with two hundred other townspeople. I didn't feel like waiting around, so I left my keys and more then enough money to cover my bill. The news conference ended just as I got to my car.

Drake saw me and hollered across the parking lot, "Hey, mister!" He ran toward me.

Instead of answering, I quickly tossed my bag into the backseat of my car. I ignored him and jumped into the front seat of the Mustang just as he got to my door. I nearly ran over him as I backed out of the parking spot. Drake quickly got out of my path and I was on the road again. The only positive part of this traumatic episode was that I got a much earlier start than I would have otherwise.

I was in Maine in no time. Since I was five hours ahead of schedule, I decided to drive up to Portland. I felt good about the time I was making.

There was a factory there that made carnival rides. I assumed that was where Boris was headed.

I drove to the main factory office. There were about twenty people sitting behind desks, sketching. They were designing future carnival rides. They looked like rides that we would never have even dreamed about. *Oh, to be a kid again!*

A stocky, bald-headed man saw me. "What can I do for you?" he asked. I showed him Boris' picture.

"Oh sure. That guy picked up a new ride two days ago—The Jumper. You must not be watching the news," he responded, a bit surprised I was not up on the local news.

"What do you mean?" I asked.

The bald-headed man shifted his toothpick to the other side of his mouth. "The State Police found a dead man found in the semi-truck yesterday. It wasn't the guy in that picture," he continued. "Funny thing, though."

"What?" I asked.

"That new ride? The Jumper? It was missing."

I asked him if there were any carnivals in town.

"Let me think," he responded thoughtfully. "Just a minute. Let me get my log book," he added as he walked away. He was gone for several minutes, so I wandered around the lobby looking at the gallery of rides pictured on the walls. Some of them dated back to the early part of the century. He finally came back with a book that listed all of the permanent carnivals in the U.S. There were even listings of notable carnivals in other countries.

"Here, take that with you," he said handing me a paper copy of current carnival listings.

"Thank you, sir," I said appreciatively and extended my hand.

I decided to head to the closest carnival. Upon arriving, I walked around the grounds looking at the various rides. I stopped at one that I recognized in one of the pictures on the wall back at the factory. I asked the midget managing that ride who was in charge of the carnival. He replied that Plinks was in charge, and if I wanted to talk to him I would have to go to the Rocket Ship ride. *Well, that's just great!* I wasn't ready for more of this outer space stuff.

I soon found Plinks and introduced myself. ""What can I do for you, Joe?" Plinks asked. I showed him Boris' picture.

"Sure, I know him," Plinks replied. He gave me a good deal on a new ride. He said he was closing his carnival in New York City." Plinks went on to say that he got The Jumper for a mere ten grand. "That was a steal. I can make my money back in just a few months."

"Well, I hate to tell you, but that ride was stolen," I replied carefully.

"Mr. Petrov had all the paper work, including the title," Plinks said defensively. "And the title was in his name."

"You can keep the ride for all I care," I responded with a wave of dismissal. "I just want to find Boris Petrov."

Carefully considering his next words, Plinks said slowly, "I was heading to my office when I overheard Boris on the pay phone asking when the next train to Morristown, Vermont, was scheduled to leave."

Excited to get this next lead—my luck really had changed—I waved a goodbye to Plinks. I got back into my Mustang and headed toward Vermont.

CHAPTER NINE

I drove all day with no break. I was hungry, and a rib-eye steak sounded perfect. I should have asked Plink where the nearest restaurant was. I drove for a bit and was just passing a large horse ranch when my Mustang sputtered and died. Maybe Billy wasn't quite the mechanic I had hoped.

A lady who looked to be about thirty years old came riding by on a black stallion. I had gotten out of my car and was standing next to the open hood that was spewing steam.

"Boy are you in a pickle," she said, smiling at me.

"I sure am." I answered, shaking my head. "I'm Joe Craig. Am I ever glad to see you!"

She introduced herself as Maggie and offered her help. I told her that my car had been running great up to this point. "I don't know what happened."

"It's not the car, Joe, it's the heat. In case you haven't noticed, it's a hundred degrees out here," "Your car needs a rest. You've probably been running it too hard." With a knowing look, she added, "I can imagine you could do with a bit of a rest yourself."

Yes, a break from this heat would be more than welcome. I had no option but to follow. I walked next to the stallion as Maggie led the way to a big colonial style house.

She tied her horse to a hitching post and introduced me. "Joe, this is Sparks. Sparks, meet Joe." Sparks whinnied his hello. Feeling just a bit silly, I acknowledged the horse and reached out to pet him. Maggie smiled and invited me to sit on her front porch.

The porch encased the entire front side of the house. There were two swings, one on each end of the porch. A table and chairs added a homey touch. I could tell this was a favorite place to relax. An elderly man, rocking in a chair to the left of the front door, eyed me with a detached curiosity.

Maggie introduced the old man as her grandfather. I said hello to him, but there was no response. Maggie excused herself and said she would get us a couple of beers. As soon as Maggie left the porch, the old man said, "They're here, they're here, they're here." He stopped as soon as Maggie returned with the beers.

"Oh, Gramps," Maggie chided as she handed me a bottle. "You'll need to excuse my grandfather. He keeps seeing spaceships. He says they fly overhead late at night and use search lights like they are hunting for something... or someone."

My heart pounded just a bit harder as her words reminded me of my own experiences with these spaceships. Obviously, Maggie had not had a personal encounter with them or watched much news lately.

We were enjoying the cold beers and casual conversation when a man drove up to the house. He got out of the truck and walked toward the porch where he greeted Maggie and Gramps warmly. He then turned to me and waited for an introduction.

Maggie introduced the man as Tyler, one of the men who kept the ranch running. I stood up and shook his hand.

"You called me to check on a car, Miss Maggie?" Tyler asked, removing his hat and turning his eyes toward her.

"Yes, Tyler," Maggie nodded. "Would you be so kind as to check out Joe's car? It died on him an hour or so ago. See if the car will start. If not, see if you can figure out what's wrong with it. It's the Mustang sitting on the side of the road at the end of the driveway. You can't miss it," she said wryly.

"Yes, ma'am, Miss Maggie," Tyler said. He returned his hat to its rightful place and walked back to his truck.

"He's such a gentleman," Maggie said as Tyler walked out of earshot. "It's my loss that he's happily married," she chuckled wistfully as if to say the good ones are already taken.

She went on to say that her grandfather built this ranch from nothing during the Great Depression.

"Gramps made his money selling firewood to the locals." She waved her hand toward the large stand of trees to the north of the house. "Sometimes they paid him money, but most of the time he traded the wood for food or help on the ranch. We have raised just about every kind of animal known to man. Gramps was always game to try anything. Now we primarily raise horses."

"My parents died in a car wreck when my sister Kitti and I were very young. Gramps took us in even though Grammy was gone. It was a challenge for sure, but he survived us!" Maggie laughed and shot a warm look in Gramps' direction.

"Our ranch has become the size of a small town." Her eyes gazed proudly at the property that spread as far as the eye could see. "As discouraged landowners bailed out of the ranching and farming business, we were able to buy them out. There just wasn't enough water to go around," Maggie explained. "And drilling for more water was so very expensive…sorry, here I am, just rambling on."

I thought Maggie was a nice person and a quite a talker. "If I weren't on this case… way too much going on to start thinking like that," I chided myself.

I heard a truck coming up the driveway. When I looked up, I saw my Mustang being towed. Tyler's Dodge Ram was pulling my car into a big metal shed. I wondered what he would find. I couldn't help but wonder if the Mustang, too, was a victim of those alien spaceships.

CHAPTER TEN

It wasn't long before Tyler was back at the front porch. He acknowledged me with a nod of the head, but it was Maggie that he addressed. "Miss Maggie, the Mustang has a cracked water pump."

He turned to face me and said, almost apologetically, "It will take a few days to get a new one out to the ranch. I'll get on it right away."

"Thanks, Tyler," Maggie said as he stepped off the porch and headed back to his office in the shop.

"Well, Joe, it looks like you're stuck with us for a couple of days, at least," Maggie said in a tone that showed no remorse for my situation. "Now, enough about me. What's your story, Joe? We have some time, so we may as well get to know each other!"

I wasn't used to being put on the spot, but I really

didn't mind telling Maggie my story. For some reason, I was rather pleased that she was interested enough to ask.

I expressed my gratitude for her help, and then I went on to tell her what I was doing here. I tried to tell the story in a nutshell, leaving out some of the details that might make me look crazy or inept. I left out the parts about the monsters, the girls from the future giving me truth coins, and the spaceships. I also didn't mention tripping, ramming Boris' car, or my missing molar. I tried to make it sound like I was an average detective on an average case. At the same time, for some reason, I wanted Maggie to be impressed.

Zorko had been reading all morning and was finally relieved to get to the part where Joe meets Maggie. He could tell that there was something different about Maggie now that she had met Joe. In the years that he had been studying her, he had never seen her interested in a man. She was always too independent. Maybe this Joe had to be part of the story of Maggie. He needed to finish up here and get back to Sagitar. Zorko picked up Joe's journal and continued reading.

When I got to the part of my story where my car quit in front of her house, she smiled and asked if I wanted another beer. "And you do this for a living?" Shaking her head, she said bluntly, "You look like you've traveled some hard miles yourself, and could stand some freshening up." She must have seen the dismay on my face because she added, "I need to check on my horses, but I want to hear more about your cases when you're rested. The horses are stabled near the guesthouse. Do you need anything from your car? Tyler can bring it to you."

"Just a small bag in the back seat is all," I said, grateful for the chance to clean up.

Maggie called Tyler and walked with me to the guesthouse. It was nestled in a small wooded area behind the main house. It was actually a duplex that was designed to look like the main house. It was quite large, yet homey. You could tell she loved this place.

"People from all over the world come here to buy our stallions," Maggie said. "Saudi Arabia, Iran.

Australia. We do all we can to make them comfortable. That's how we make a living," she grinned openly.

Tyler tapped on the door and set the bag on the floor. She took that as her cue to leave. She put her hand on my arm and said, "I will leave you alone for a while, Joe. Dinner is at seven."

I felt a bit flustered. *What is happening to me?* I told her I looked forward to a bit of good home cooking and would be there on time. I watched television for a while until I got sleepy. I haven't exactly had many good nights. I stretched out on the bed and took a short nap. Or at least I thought it was short until I looked at the clock. It was after six. I quickly unpacked my bag and headed to the shower. Promptly at seven (I didn't want to look too eager), I went to the main house and knocked on the door.

A wonderful aroma greeted me just as Maggie yelled for me to come on in. "I'm in the living room. Dinner is nearly ready. Would you like a drink before we eat?" A maid, Nellie, was putting the finishing touches on dinner. I was nearly finished with my drink when a younger version of Maggie and two little girls walked in.

"Sorry we're late," the young woman said breathlessly and with a curious stare at Joe. "The girls insisted on wearing the pink sparkly shoes you gave them, and, of course, couldn't remember where they had last taken them off."

Maggie smiled and gave the girls each a hug. "Perfect timing," she said. "I think dinner is ready," She gestured Joe to a seat.

"Thank you. It sure looks good, Maggie, just like Thanksgiving— turkey, mashed potatoes, even corn on the cob. I haven't had much home cooking these past few months."

Gramps was already at the head of the table. Maggie introduced the woman as her sister, Kitti, and the two little girls as Kara and Tara. Kitti added that they were five years old and definitely double trouble. They were going to start Kindergarten in the fall, which would give her a few hours to herself. Kitti was as forthcoming as Maggie and continued, "My husband died right after the kids were born, so they've never had a father. It was a difficult time and Maggie didn't want me to work. She knew the girls would need a full-time mother." Kitti shot an affectionate look in Maggie's direction. "I don't know what I would do without her." You could tell they were close.

After dinner, Maggie left the room to help Nellie get dessert and coffee.

Maggie came back into the kitchen with apple pie alamode. We all talked business and politics until the two little girls got restless.

Kitti stood up said it was time to get the girls home. She thanked her sister for dinner, said goodbye to Joe, and whispered in his ear, "Don't be surprised if it takes a while to get your car fixed."

I was sure a blush crept all the way from my feet to my hair. Maggie seemed like a great person, but I couldn't afford the time to be stuck here.

After cleaning things up a bit, Maggie invited me to go on a late night horse ride. Feeling rested from my nap, I agreed. We walked to the stables where Tyler was getting two horses ready. I wondered how Tyler had known that Maggie and I were going for a ride when I spotted the phone on the wall. Maggie was pretty sly, I thought.

Maggie gave me Spook to ride. "Gramps named him Spook," Maggie said, "because he ran cattle years ago, and the horse would always spook the cattle by trying to round them up." I took hold of Spook's reins and mounted easily. I had ridden plenty of horses before, so I was certain I could keep up with Maggie.

We took the horses on a slow gallop, mainly because

it was dark. We came up over a ridge and the horses began acting a bit nervous. Straight ahead, up in the sky, lights flashed. I immediately thought of the spaceship that I had seen earlier, but fortunately it was just a helicopter. I hoped my nervousness wasn't evident to Maggie.

"The helicopters are from the National Guard base nearby," Maggie commented.

We came across a small creek. Spook and Sparks dipped their heads into the water and took long, slow drinks. Maggie told me the creek was called Dry as a Bone Creek because it's dry most of the year. But by this time of the year, the snow had melted and run off the mountain.

While the horses were drinking their fill, I noticed a black bear strolling near the creek. "Look, Maggie," I said pointing to the bear.

Maggie said they were usually shy, but to be on the safe side, she always carried a rifle on the side of the saddle. When she pulled it out and placed it over her lap, I realized what an independent woman she was. I watched as she aimed her rifle into the air and gave the bear a warning shot. The bear looked up, saw us, and moseyed back into the woods.

After the horses had their fill of water, we rode for

another thirty minutes. I wondered where we were. It was hard to tell our location because there were tall trees on both sides of the path. We must not have been too far from civilization because a small dachshund came bounding up beside Maggie and Sparks. Maggie greeted Schotzie, asking her why she was so far from home. She went on to say that Kitti had adopted Schotzie years ago before the twins were born. After her husband died, she and the girls spent some time with Maggie on the ranch. Schotzie loved it so much Kitti didn't have the heart to keep her cooped up in a small yard. Schotzie has been a part of the ranch ever since.

The trails had gotten rougher, so after another hour of slow going, Maggie suggested we go back to the ranch. I hadn't spent much time in the saddle lately, and my backside wholeheartedly agreed! Back at the barn, Tyler took the horses. We stood out in the moonlight and chatted for a moment before Maggie said goodnight. I watched her as she walked slowly to the house. It had been a long day and I hoped sleep would come easy.

I found a cabinet stocked with all kinds of liquor. Some of the bottles looked as though they had come from some very wealthy guests that had stayed at the ranch when they came to buy horses.

I figured Maggie wouldn't mind if I had a nightcap

before turning in. I found myself wishing Maggie were still here to share one with me. I settled comfortably into a chair and turned on the television. I watched the last few minutes of a John Wayne western and then turned in.

CHAPTER ELEVEN

Even though I got up shortly after sunrise, I wasn't the only one awake. The ranch was in full swing. I walked up to the main house where Nellie had breakfast waiting on the front porch. She said Maggie was with the horses and would see me later.

I enjoyed my breakfast, refilled my coffee, and walked toward the stables where Maggie was working. She nodded a greeting, but was too intent on what she was doing to come over to where I was leaning on the fence. I spent the rest of the morning watching her train a colt. The young horse was chomping at the bit, fighting Maggie with all its strength as she tried to get him to rear up. It took the better part of the morning, but soon she had that colt doing things her way. I couldn't help but feel a deep respect for this woman.

Maggie, pleased with herself, got off the horse and

asked me if I had slept well.

"Like a baby," I smiled warmly.

She said she was finished for the day and wondered if I would like to go with her to town to run some quick errands. If we felt like it, she added, we could see an early movie.

"That would be nice," I said. It had been a long time since I had actually gone to a movie theater. I watched as Maggie handed the horse over to Tyler with instructions to wipe him down and give him a good grooming. As we got into her pickup truck, I remembered Kitti's parting remark about my car repairs. I couldn't help wonder how long it would take.

I kept her company as she stopped at the feed store, post office, and hardware store. Happy to have something to do, I helped her load supplies into the truck and fasten the tarp over them. She finished early so we decided to stop for ice cream. I had vanilla with fresh strawberries and Maggie had chocolate. We sat outside and Maggie asked again about my cases. I told her a bit about Nick, Steve and Mrs. Cryer, but left out the part about the caves and the machines from the future. I was telling her about my new house when a monster walked into the ice cream parlor. Not wanting a conflict with him, I put my necklace under my shirt. I could feel my hands begin to sweat a bit, and I hoped my wariness didn't show. It was time to go anyway. Maggie didn't believe Gramps and the reports of aliens, so I knew I needed to keep quiet about what I had just seen.

Maggie chose a romance movie—I hoped I could stay awake through it! We were just getting our seats when a man grabbed Maggie's drink and tossed it in her face. I started to scuffle with the man when security intervened. I began to explain what had happened when security told me they had seen the whole thing. The man was escorted out, and Maggie excused herself to the Ladies room to clean up. I followed behind her to make sure she was okay.

When she came out, she said she was not going to let that man ruin her time, so we went back to our seats. Management was waiting with an apology, a complimentary pair of tickets, and another drink for Maggie. After we sat down, she explained the story behind what had just happened. She said the man, Jake, used to work for her, but she had to fire him.

"He treated the horses badly," she said. "I caught him using whips when he trained them. He knew I didn't hold to that kind of treatment. I was so furious I pulled the rifle from my saddle and almost shot him on the spot. If it hadn't been for Gramps, I would have shot him for sure. Gramps grabbed the rifle from me and told me to go inside and get the man's pay. When I came back outside, Jake was on the ground. I thought Gramps had shot him!"

"I'm sure glad you didn't shoot the guy," I said. I surprised myself by adding, "Otherwise, we wouldn't have met." Maggie gave me a sidelong glance that was both surprised and pleased.

During the movie, I surprised myself again. I put my arm around Maggie. I felt her move just a bit closer to me, and that felt nice. I didn't want to admit it, but the movie wasn't half bad. Maybe it was the company.

After the movie, Maggie asked me if I was up to dancing. *Where does she get all of her energy?*

"I'm pretty light on my feet," I bragged, showing her my moves. She laughed and we headed to the only nightspot in town. We had a beer and slow danced to a few songs. Maggie was a good dance partner, and I felt myself wishing the evening would not end.

CHAPTER TWELVE

The next morning, I noticed Maggie at the stables talking to Tyler. From what I could see, Tyler looked upset. All I could hear was, "No, that's not right, Miss Maggie."

"Do it anyway," she said as she stomped off.

Later, when I was sitting on Maggie's front porch, I heard Gramps arguing with Maggie about the price of apples. Gramps was complaining that apples were fifty-five cents for only three pounds.

"Ridiculous," Gramps hollered. 'Instead of raising horses, I'm going to grow apples."

"No you are not, Gramps." Maggie hollered back.

"Well, we should." Gramps stomped out to the front porch with an apple in one hand and a pocket-knife in the other.

He turned to me and asked, "Joe, do you have apple farms in Indiana?"

"We sure do, Gramps. Apple growing is one of the top cash crops back home." I hoped my comment wouldn't set him off more. I didn't want to cause more aggravation for Maggie. Just then, Tyler hollered at me from the shop. I saw that he was working on my Mustang, so I excused myself and headed his way.

"Good news, Mr. Joe. The new water pump just came. I got it all installed and it works fine." Tyler then hid his head under the hood and added quietly, "Unfortunately, though, I ran a big screwdriver through the radiator. I'm really sorry, Mr. Joe. Of course, I'll pay for a new one. I've already ordered it."

I could tell he felt horrible about the situation.

"Thank you, but that's not necessary. You're doing all of the work and I appreciate that," I replied shaking my head. I knew I should be upset because I didn't think it was an accident. *Why would you need to use such a big screwdriver on a water pump?* I heard Kitti's words again, "Don't be surprised if it takes a while to get your car fixed."

Tyler assured me it would be finished in only a few

more days. There wasn't much I could do about my situation, but all I could think about was Boris getting farther and farther away.

Maggie was waiting for me at the guesthouse. "Tyler will fix your car as fast as he can. I know he feels responsible for you losing more time."

We talked a bit about Boris and then she grabbed my arm and suggested we go swimming after she finished tending the horses. I hesitated but then thought swimming might be a good way for me to cool off. I offered to help her with the horses and we were soon finished. I ran to the guesthouse and quickly changed into my trunks.

We drove a few miles to a small lake just west of the ranch. It was a clean little lake with a small dock. We walked along the shore for a few minutes and then slowly edged our way into the sun-warmed water. I have to admit the water did feel good, and Maggie looked pretty darn good in a swimsuit.

We were both good swimmers and enjoyed a leisurely swim across the lake and back. Refreshed but exhausted, we spread our towels on the warm sand. We stretched out to let the sun dry us off. Maggie closed her eyes. I watched her as she basked in the warmth of the sun. She was an amazing woman—strong, yet she had a vulnerability that made me want to protect her.

We were dry in no time. Maggie opened her eyes and caught me watching her. She blushed just a bit and said quickly that Nellie had packed a picnic lunch for us. I was good and hungry after that swim, so I corralled my thoughts and got the basket out of the car. We sat at the picnic table and enjoyed our sandwiches and beer. I mentioned to her that I had heard her arguing with Tyler. He didn't seem like the type that would argue with a lady, let alone his boss.

Maggie's face turned beet red. "I'm sorry," she said. "I know I put Tyler in a real bind. I asked him to make sure your car didn't get fixed for a few more days. I have never done anything like that before." She hung her head and whispered quietly, "I just didn't want you to leave."

After a few seconds, she lifted her head and looked me in the eyes. "Your radiator was an accident. I asked Tyler to hide the water pump for a few days. Noble Tyler said it wasn't right to do that to you. He was upset with me, and when he was installing the water pump, his hand slipped and the screwdriver went clear through the radiator. I'm so sorry, Joe."

I reached over and took her hand and told her that I liked her, too. I gave her a tentative kiss. At this point, I had mixed emotions. I knew I needed to leave, but I was more than a little glad to spend extra time with Maggie. She returned my kiss and then said softly "We'd better go."

CHAPTER THIRTEEN

That night after dinner, I hung around talking to Gramps on the front porch while Maggie finished ranch business. Gramps acted like he wanted to say something that he didn't want Maggie to hear. He kept looking in the direction of her office and shaking his head.

"Joe, I want to show you something. Want to come with me for a quick ride?"

"Sure thing," I agreed curiously.

Gramps hollered to Maggie that we were going for a little ride. We walked to the barn and got into an old pickup. I was sure that it was as old as the ranch itself. I wondered how an old truck like that even stayed together. *Did Gramps use bailing wire or duct tape?* It didn't look like much, but the old truck could sure run. The engine had been well maintained. This must be how Gramps spent his days.

We drove to a small canyon on the property a fair distance from the house. Gramps made sure we couldn't be seen. He drove to the edge of the canyon and had me look down. I was shocked at what I saw. There were little flying saucers flitting all around the canyon.

All they seemed to be doing was going around and around in circles. I could see dust flying, but not much else.

Gramps whispered, "I told you they were here." A shiver ran down my spine as I realized these tiny flying saucers were the same shape and size as the ones I had barely escaped earlier in the week.

"What are they doing?" I asked.

"I think they are digging for minerals. I'm not sure, though," Gramps said. "They're here almost every night. I called the sheriff once, but he just ignored me. He told me he knew all about the spaceships. It was a secret government project, and I was to leave them alone. I figured the Sheriff was either trying to humor me or he was an alien himself.

"But I knew differently. I saw the mother ship," Gramps said quietly. He gave me a quick glance to see if I, too, was humoring him.

All of a sudden, with no warning, the small ships shot off into space.

"Keep this spaceship stuff to yourself, Joe." Gramps continued his story. "A year ago, I was in this canyon, at this very spot, planting trees. It was early evening and just getting dark. I saw a big space ship hover overhead, its lights searching the canyon. After a few minutes, smaller ones came out of the large ship and began circling around the mother ship. About fifteen minutes later, they were gone. The spaceships have been coming back ever since. I have no idea what they want. I'm worried, Joe. I don't believe it has anything to do with secret government projects."

We rode home in silence. I wondered if there was a connection between these spaceships and the monsters I saw whenever I wore my truth necklace. I hoped I wouldn't have nightmares again tonight.

CHAPTER FOURTEEN

The next morning before breakfast, Maggie sat on the porch swing. It seemed natural to take her hand while we talked quietly. I felt like a schoolboy again. I was almost glad that Tyler had punctured my radiator.

She had to leave for a town council meeting, so we decided I would come in later for a lunch date. Tyler was picking up supplies in town late morning, so he could drop me off at the library. Maggie's meeting was at City Hall just down the street.

After she left, I sat alone on the swing thinking about her and wondered just where this relationship would go once I left. Since I wasn't at all used to sitting, I got a bit restless. I took a slow walk around the property and ended up by the shop. Tyler looked up from his work and nodded a greeting. I waved back and continued on to the guesthouse.

I had an hour to kill before I needed to leave, so I turned on the television to see what was happening in the rest of the country. The story of the day was about the arrest of a leading mobster in Lower Manhattan. The police had reliable witnesses that testified they saw the Abbott family mob boss Barnabas Abbott, alias Big Foot, shoot two rival family members. The city was bracing for retaliation against the Abbott Family syndicate.

I watched the local weather, but when the sports came on I decided I had seen enough. I had been too busy to keep up on any of the teams and wasn't interested in listening to any more of the game updates.

Tyler tapped on my door and stepped in. He was ready to head into town. I grabbed my jacket and wallet and met him at the shop. He was still feeling guilty about the radiator and had a difficult time looking me in the eye. I explained that Maggie had told me the whole story and that I had no hard feelings. He was still quiet, but when we got to the library, he shook hands with me and nodded his thanks.

It was a beautiful morning, so I decided to sit outside on the bench. I needed to plan my next steps. Boris was getting farther and farther away. I was used to being on top of everything and was feeling like I had lost control. It had taken me these last two years to put to rest the case involving Pam and Sherry. I dealt in facts, or used to; but now everything seemed to be spiraling out of control. I wasn't even sure what to do about Maggie. I had never been torn between my job and a woman before. I was lost in thought when someone sat down beside me. Absentmindedly, I looked up. Pam and Sherry smiled a hello.

I'm not sure I will ever get used to these random appearances. I greeted the girls back and asked what brought them here, of all places.

"You," they replied in unison.

"We see you are in somewhat of a dilemma," Sherry added, a questioning look on her face.

"We are, too," said Pam. "We aren't supposed to upset the future by interfering in the present, but we can see some trouble ahead."

"Trouble for whom?" I asked. "For me? I'm already in trouble! But of course you already know that!"

Pam and Sherry exchanged knowing looks, but didn't say anything for a moment. "We know you are getting pretty involved with Maggie. You wonder where your relationship with her will go." As Pam talked, Sherry kept her eyes low. That didn't look good, but I would worry about the future in the future. "You are also concerned about finding Boris. We might be able to help you out there without really interfering. We know Boris is in Seattle right now. He won't be there for long, so given your current car issue, we thought we could pass that information along. And remember—he likes the water and has a love for strong drink."

Just as quickly as they came, the girls were gone. I briefly wondered what made them decide to help me out. I had to admit it made me a bit nervous thinking that I was still on their radar. I would worry about that later, too. Now I just had to figure out how to get to Seattle. I gave a call to Washington D.C. and filled them in on what was happening. I told them I was heading to Seattle as Boris had been spotted there.

After a brief discussion, I returned to the problem at hand. "How do I tell Maggie?" I said aloud.

"Tell Maggie what?" she said, suddenly appearing by my side. *What was it with women always sneaking up on me?*

I've always thought it best just to say what was on my mind, so I did. I did leave out the part about Pam and Sherry, though. I told her I had just had a conversation with D.C., and that I had to get to Seattle because I had a new lead on Boris' whereabouts.

Tears began to well up in her eyes and my resolve began to wane. "How long will you be gone?"

Here I go. "Maggie, I know we've only know each other for a few days. It may be presumptuous of me to say this, but I haven't felt like this about a woman for a very long time. I'm not a kid with a crush. This is different. I reached out to her, and she held me as tightly as I held her. "I will be back as soon as I put this guy behind bars. Besides, my Mustang is here, and you know how I feel about her!"

Maggie managed a small laugh as tears rolled down her cheeks. "So much for trying to keep you here," she sniffled. "That's what I get!" She gave me a long, sweet kiss mixed with tears. We had a quick lunch and went back to the ranch to pack before she drove me to the airport.

CHAPTER FIFTEEN

It was a long day, but by midnight I had arrived at the SeaTac airport. I took a cab to downtown Seattle. Finding a hotel room was easy—my cab driver knew his way around. I had promised Maggie that I would call her, but I figured it could wait until morning. She knew I was getting in late.

I went to the bar and ordered a drink before settling in. I don't like to drink on the airplane, so I was ready for a nightcap by the time I got to the hotel. I still had a lot to think about. I never seemed to have time to get one thought settled before another crowded it out.

As I sat there with a cold drink in my hands, I saw some guy furtively looking around. Being in this kind of business requires you to always be aware of those around you. This guy just looked guilty. I watched him for a few seconds, and then I saw his hand dart quickly from his side to a wallet sitting on one of the tables where a gentleman with a white cane was sitting. I quickly intervened, grabbing the would-be thief by the back of his long, greasy hair. The thief, surprised but not deterred, spun around and pulled out a three-inch knife. I grabbed the hand that held the knife and got cut for my reward. My hand began to drip with blood, but I, too, was not going to be deterred. Boy, this guy is strong, I thought, giving the thief a hook to the face. He quickly recovered from the blow and grabbed me by the back of my hair and slammed my face into the table. I grabbed a beer bottle, reared up, and smashed it onto the thief's head. He fell to the floor groaning, but didn't get back up.

The police arrested us both. I tried to explain, but I was told to tell my story down at the station. I guess it was my luck that the only one who could corroborate my story didn't see it happen! It took far longer than it should have to get everything sorted out. They ran a check on the thief and found he had skipped bail in England and would be held for extradition.

After checking up on me, they let me go with a few strong words. The chief rubbed the back of his neck and warned me to stay out of trouble. He could see that I was who I said I was, but also could see that trouble seemed to follow me. He didn't know the half of it. It was nearly sun-up, but I was free to go.

On my way back to the hotel, we passed the waterfront. I knew Boris liked being around water, and the girls told me once that he liked to fish, so I knew that this would be a good place to start.

I was hungry, so I asked the cabbie to drop me off at a good restaurant along the bay. He said there were several, so he dropped me off near the water. I stayed on the walkway, half looking at the fishing boats and half at the restaurants. There were several large charter boats as well as several smaller boats for hire. It was there that I saw Boris. He was boarding a small boat with two other people. The sign said it was an all day fishing excursion, so I knew I must return before dark.

I enjoyed a hearty breakfast and several cups of coffee before I called another cab to take me back to my hotel. I caught a few winks and planned to call Maggie later. I slept like a baby even after several cups of caffeine.

That morning about eleven, I finally woke up enough to give Maggie a call. I could hear the excitement in her voice as she asked questions about my progress. I could see her head shake as I told her about my trip to the police station and the chief's admonition to stay out of trouble. I was glad to be able to tell her I had seen Boris because that made it easier for her to accept my being away. I also asked her to send me the three necklaces that I left on the shelf above the fireplace in her guesthouse. When she asked me why I had three identical necklaces, I told her they were gifts from a good friend and that I was to give one to Steve and one to Nick. I knew I couldn't tell her the whole truth because I had seen how she was with Gramps whenever he talked about the aliens. She agreed to overnight them to the hotel. We blew kisses and hung up with the promise of another phone call.

I had only had a couple hours sleep, and I was still tired, so I crawled back into bed. It took me a long while, though, to fall asleep. Either Maggie was taking up more of my thoughts or the caffeine had just kicked in.

I finally drifted off. I must have slept the sleep of the dead because I woke up to a very dark room. I had missed Boris' return.

I quickly dressed and called the cab to again take me out to the waterfront where I did the next best thing to catching Boris. I interviewed the fisherman that had taken him out earlier that day. He said it was the strangest thing. Boris didn't want to fish. He and the other two guys were going to the south side of town, and paying him to ferry them over was a quicker way to get there. They would miss the morning rush and would enjoy the fresh air at the same time. I thanked him for the information; I knew I would be heading to the south side of Seattle tomorrow afternoon.

The next morning, a package was waiting for me at the front desk. Maggie had sent the necklaces. She had also enclosed a photo of herself standing next to my Mustang. A note said, "Your two best girls."

I ate a quick breakfast and grabbed a coffee to go. I put on one of the necklaces and then stashed the other two in the hotel safe. The first thing I had to do was rent another car. I found a 1967 Mustang. It felt good to be behind the wheel of a great car again. I checked the map the salesman had given me and headed to the south side of town.

I hardly knew where to begin, but I figured I would start where the tourist attractions were. Boris seemed to like that sort of thing. I canvassed the area with no luck. I needed a break, so I crossed the street to a somewhat seedy looking bar. It was dark inside, and I remembered what the girls had said about Boris and liquor.

 I sat where I could watch the door. It was almost too much to hope for, but Pam and Sherry always knew what they were talking about. They could see the future, after all. I was about to give up when Boris and two other Russians came through the door. I almost dropped my drink. *Stay calm.* I quietly walked to the pay phone in the back by the restrooms. I was thankful for the dark room. I called the police chief and, thankfully, he remembered our conversation. He also remembered the cut on my hand. He said to sit tight and to not approach the men. He would call it into the local precinct and they would send someone right over.

Boris was now leaning on the bar. He ordered a beer for himself and the other two guys. I tried to get a bit closer to him, but he reeked of a week's worth of sweat and stunk worse than a wet hog in August. Being from Indiana, I knew what I was talking about. "And get my friend here one, too," Boris said, putting his arm around my shoulders.

"Thanks," I said trying not to look Boris in the face.

Boris squinted at me in the dark. He stared at me for a moment with his brow furrowed and eyes narrowed, "Hey, I know you. You're the guy who tried to run me off the road."

I tried to get away, but his arm tightened around my shoulders. The next thing I knew, I was eating his fist. I fell sideways, but recovered quickly enough to swing back at Boris with all I had. He fell backwards into the jukebox hard enough to make the record skip. I pulled out my .38 and told Boris to stay on the floor. That was the last thing I remembered until I woke up with a splitting headache and the police standing over me.

"I thought the chief asked you to wait," the officer chided.

"Boris recognized me," I said, rubbing my head. I looked at the broken glass all around me and added, "I guess one of Boris' friends didn't like his beer."

"Well, Boris got away, but we have the other two. We're heading to the station right now. You can come along if you like. The chief said to offer you every consideration we could," the officer in charge said to me.

Down at the station, the two Russians told me they were part of an organization that helped other Russian immigrants get settled in the U.S. "We're hard-working people, and we try to take care of our own," one of the arrested Russian told me.

"We didn't know who you were or that Boris was a fugitive," another added. "Had we known, we would have turned Boris in ourselves."

I believed them both for now and said that I

wouldn't press charges. The police let both Russians go.

The officer in charge assured me every police officer available was looking for Boris. If he were still in Seattle, the police would find him.

There wasn't much I could do right now, so I decided to take a drive around the city. I went to the waterfront hoping I might get a glimpse of Boris. I could see a lot of people walking around, but no monsters. I called them monsters, because I couldn't find another word to describe them. I knew they were aliens, but that was what everyone called them. These aliens were different. They were aliens but acted and looked like humans to the average person. Without this necklace, they were just as human as I was. With the necklace on, I could see them morph into monsters. That's it! I would call them Morphs.

I enjoyed my drive around Seattle. It helped clear my thoughts and get my mind off this headache from the blow in the bar.

The beauty of the great northwest impressed me. On the flight in, I had looked down from the plane to see the moon shining on these magnificent mountains. Even though it was dark, I could see the magnitude of the range. They stretched for hundreds of miles.

The pilot rattled off their names, but to me, they were all one mountain.

I reluctantly went back to my hotel room, got the pictures of Boris, and had copies made. I then spent the next couple of days hunting for the elusive fugitive. I handed out flyers with his picture plastered all over but had no luck. I decided to check back in at the police station to see if they had anything on him. The captain was there working with two other detectives on another case. He saw me and walked over to where I was talking with the Sargent and told me that there was nothing new on Boris. He would call me as soon as there was a lead.

CHAPTER SIXTEEN

True to his word, the next morning the captain called to say that someone fitting Boris' description had been spotted west of Salem, Oregon. It was in a small town called Grand Ronde.

I was anxious to get going—this case was dragging on way too long. I packed up my things and checked out of the hotel. I drove to the police station to thank the captain for calling me. He wished me luck and handed me a map with the directions to Salem highlighted.

I stopped for a big cup of coffee and headed toward I-5. I knew this would be another relaxing drive through some beautiful country. I wasn't disappointed. I wished Maggie were with me, but I settled for singing along with the radio.

I saw a **Gas Food and Lodging Next Three Exits**

sign and glanced down at my gas gauge. I was nearly out. I exited the freeway. I filled my tank and got another large coffee to go. This must be a popular truck stop because there were a dozen semi-trucks and a store that sold more tools then Sears.

I was about to leave when a bus pulled in and blocked my exit. I wasn't in any particular hurry, but I was afraid they would be a long time. I looked up and saw that the bus was full of Morphs. They were all Morphs, including the driver.

Except for their height and weight, they all looked the same. I was surprised by one of the Morphs, however. She was beautiful. She was surrounded by more Morphs, almost like they were protecting her. She was being watched very closely. Was she like the queen bee of the morph people? Although she was green, she was a beautiful green. She had long, brown, braided hair. She also had human ears and fingers. I was puzzled by the different looks of the Morph men and women. I wondered how the women could be attracted to such monstrous looking men. Maybe on her planet was she's the ugly one. Maybe, I thought, the Morphs, unlike us, didn't have attractions to the opposite sex. I was kind of surprised by my calm thinking. I should be more frightened than I was. *Was I becoming used to all of this space craziness?*

Even though I could have inched my way out, I decided to stay put and wait for them to leave. I needed to figure out how they fit into my life. Pam and Sherry had given me the necklaces for a reason. About thirty minutes later, they were all back on the bus and headed south. I followed them, keeping a good distance behind.

Four hours later, the bus took the first Salem exit; it didn't stop in Salem, but headed for the Oregon coast. I wasn't sure how much gas the bus had, but my car was running on fumes.

I stopped for gas and quickly got back on the road. I caught up in no time. About thirty miles from Salem, the bus took a right down a gravel road. I stayed well behind the bus, hoping not to be spotted by the bus driver. Suddenly, the bus slowed down. I pulled into the next driveway and watched as two men opened the gate to a farm. The bus disappeared down a long driveway. I got out of my car and followed on foot. The men closed the gate and headed to the house.

I wrote down the address. One thing I learned early in my line of work was to always carry a lot of pencils and notepads. Pens were unreliable; if they didn't leak, they ran out of ink. On the other hand, you could use a pencil until you were sliding the lead with your fingers.

I headed back to the main road. I had seen a resort and figured I would get a room there. I checked into my room and the first thing I did was unpack and order laundry service. I hadn't had much to eat today, so I decided I needed a good dinner. The resort had several nice restaurants and a café or two. I decided on one of the nicer ones, and I was seated quickly. A friendly but sassy waitress named Willie took my order. Willie was very efficient, making sure I didn't run out of whiskey and coke. I ordered the steak with fries and a small salad. The food was spectacular, as was the waitress. I could barely finish my dinner and decided I needed to move around a bit. I had been sitting all day and my head was in need of fresh air. As I walked around the resort, all I could think about was Maggie. I needed to think about Boris.

Grand Ronde was a beautiful area—very green and peaceful. After a long walk, I headed back to the lobby. It was large with several rooms off the west end. I noticed some men sitting around a table and realized it was a poker game. Now, I pride myself in being a pretty good player, so I waited until someone folded and asked if I could join. A gentleman pulled out the empty chair and I sat down.

Almost immediately, a server came my way asking if

I wanted a drink. I figured a nice cup of coffee would be the best thing for the moment. She introduced herself as Jennifer and kept coming around making sure I had everything I needed. I wasn't doing too badly, so after a few hands, I asked her to bring me a whiskey and coke. I won the first game and tipped her well. I continued to win but eventually decided I should stop while I was ahead—and before someone got too irritated. It was late and I was tired, so I headed up to my room. On my way, I saw Jennifer and we struck up a conversation. She showed me pictures of her son Mason. I could tell she was a proud mother, so I gave her a hundred dollar bill and told her to put it into his savings.

I continued on to my room and tried to plan tomorrow, but thinking was difficult after all that whiskey. I had two issues to think about. I had started out just needing to find Boris. He was my main priority. But these Morph people were becoming so deeply integrated into my search for him, that I could not ignore their presence. I needed to figure out where they fit into the plan. Since Pam and Sherry had given me this necklace, I couldn't ignore them. Both mysteries seemed more complicated than I could handle. I wasn't sure if I could solve both cases alone. This was a new feeling for me, and I didn't like not having total control. That was why I was so good at my job.

I knew I couldn't go to the police about the Morph people. Who would believe me? They would lock me up in a mental institution. I needed a plan to get into that farmhouse where all the Morphs from the bus were hiding. At least I knew where they were—it was Boris I couldn't find.

Zorko stopped reading Joe's Journal for a moment. This Boris was becoming a major sore spot in Joe's life and Zorko wanted to know a bit more about him. He picked up Boris' journal and began to read.

I was suddenly awake. I could see hundreds of people who had been put on the cover of a book. People were screaming, but they couldn't move. I, too, could not move. I was on one of the book covers.

Another monster was force-feeding them from small syringes. A monster picked me up off the book. I screamed and swung my fists to no avail. I felt a tube slide down my throat. The monsters forced me to eat and then I was placed back on the book.

"We all hung from the ceiling by clamps connected to the book covers. A door opened and I could see the darkness outside. The space ship was still on earth. A loud siren filled the air and all the books fell to the floor. Our straps came loose and we fell off the book covers. We ran around like ants, not knowing which way to go. One man headed toward the door, so I yelled for others to follow. I figured I would be much harder to catch if I was in a crowd.

"Once outside the spaceship, I grew back to my normal size. Monsters were everywhere. I was now their size and able to better defend myself. I grabbed a monster by the back of the neck and shoved my fist into his mouth. Monster teeth flew everywhere. He landed hard and I watched with pleasure as he turned into a pile of dust.

Another monster grabbed me from behind. The dead monster dropped his weapon, so I broke free and grabbed the gun and pulled the trigger. A red beam of light shot out and disintegrated the second monster.

I didn't have much time. I was in a rocky area. I knew it would be risky to climb the cliffs, but I didn't have much of a choice. I cut myself on the sharp rocks and hoped that my blood wouldn't leave a scent trail for these horrible creatures to follow. I made it to the top of the cliffs and ran out on the narrow country road. Up ahead, I saw a ranch house.

I could hear the monsters calling, "Boris, Boris, where are you?" They weren't far behind. Then I saw a barn, but it was empty. It had nothing that would help me escape. Then I ran to a shed where mechanic's tools were thrown about. It was the Ford Mustang, though, that caught my eye. I opened the door. Yes! The keys were still in the ignition. I slid into the driver's seat and turned the key. Never had the sound of a purring motor been so sweet. I put the Mustang into gear and spun out of the shed. I glanced quickly in the rear view mirror and did not see any monsters following me.

I headed toward the highway. I could see small spaceships overhead like they were following me. I came upon a wooded area where I could easily hide the car. I walked half a mile and hid in some brush like a deer and waited for morning.

I knew the spaceships wouldn't be out during the day, so at daylight I cautiously headed back to the car. I drove to the nearest train depot. I was a bit at a loss until a hobo showed me a freight train that was headed to Appleton City. I hated giving up my fine ride, but I couldn't take the chance of being stopped in a nice Mustang like this.

Two days later, dirty and hungry, I arrived in Appleton City, Missouri. There was a homeless shelter near the freight yard and they gave me food to eat, some new clothes, and a bed. I stayed there for about a week. They helped me get a job in a factory making plastic dishes. The pay was okay, so I hoped I would soon have enough money to skip the country.

I needed to keep to myself. I did make a few friends and confided in them. I told them about being in a small Oregon town on a deserted farm, asleep in one of the bedrooms. I told them the ugliest monster imaginable woke me up. I told them that the monster pulled out this devise, aimed it at me, and the next thing I knew I was on his space ship. My friends were drunk at the time, so I wasn't sure if they believed me or not. I'm sure they didn't. If it had not happened to me, I wouldn't have believed it either.

I needed to lay low, so that meant no more getting into trouble or drinking. But that didn't last long. Some guy, who has been after me for weeks, showed up at my work. He wanted to take me to the Feds so I had no choice but to grab his gun and shoot him. Now I'm on the run again. No one believes me and I'm afraid for my life. I am writing this journal so if I disappear, someone will know where to look. I know I am being tracked by the F.B.I., but I fear aliens are also tracking me.

Monsters? Aliens? Zorko was a bit put off by Boris' crudeness. Sagitar offered so much more than these humans deserved. Boris was inconsequential. He needed to know more about Joe and Maggie.

Zorko put down Boris' journal and continued to read from Joe's.

CHAPTER SEVENTEEN

I missed Maggie and decided to give her a call. I knew it would be really late there, but I called anyway. Surprisingly, she didn't answer but Gramps did.

"Hi, Joe," Gramps answered. I asked politely how he was doing. "Joe, I'm glad you called. Things are picking up in the canyon. There are twice as many of those little flying saucers. They must be removing part of the canyon, because this morning it looked deeper than normal. I set a benchmark in the canyon to see if I'm right."

"Good idea, Gramps. Keep me posted."

"Will do, Joe. Here's Maggie."

"Hi Joe, Maggie said softly. She filled me in on the happenings there at the ranch. She had guests from Saudi Arabia who were interested in a couple of her stallions for breeding. They offered $200,000 apiece, but she was hoping to get more.

"Oh, and your car is fixed, Joe. Tyler takes it for a spin now and then to keep it running good. I hope that's ok. He says it needs to run regularly and I take him at his word. All I know about cars is that they get me where I need to go." Maggie rambled on for about ten more minutes. I think she was afraid that if I talked, I would say I wasn't coming back.

"I love you, Joe," Maggie surprised me by saying.

Love was a big word and I shocked myself by telling Maggie that I loved her, too. The silence that followed wasn't awkward, but was almost an exclamation point.

"I will see you very soon, Maggie."

I could imagine her fighting back tears as she said goodnight.

I had to get my mind off Maggie, so I tried to think of a way to get onto the farm where the bus was hidden. There wasn't a way to gain access legally, so I needed to come up with a way to sneak in without getting caught. I didn't want to lose another molar! I would need a gun since I lost mine in the bar fight. I also needed some dark clothes and a flashlight. And I needed some help.

I had noticed a general store just back up the highway, so I quickly headed out. I parked in the dark lot and went into the store. I picked up a flashlight, extra batteries, and a dark sweatshirt. I also threw in a pair of work gloves. As I was paying my bill, I saw a couple of hunting rifles on the wall. I asked the clerk where I could get a handgun. He looked at me carefully, as if sizing me up. He said he knew someone who could help me. I've been around the block a few times, so I figured we were doing some underground buying and selling. He kept his eyes on me the entire time he was talking. After he hung up, he said someone would be along in a moment that could help me. I told him I would wait in my car. I sat there for about fifteen minutes planning tomorrow night's excursion to the farm.

An old, beat-up sedan finally pulled into the darkest part of the parking lot. Its lights flashed on and off, and the clerk came out. After lighting up a cigarette and looking around, he came and tapped on my window. I got out of the car and followed him to the sedan. He introduced me to a shady looking character who said he could get me any handgun I wanted for five hundred dollars. I took him up on his offer and asked for a .38 Special.

He opened his trunk and removed a blanket. There was a small wooden crate with half a dozen handguns in it. He removed the .38 and said I should give it a try. The clerk had stepped about thirty feet away and put a couple of bottles on top of a stump. I took aim and hit one of the bottles, even in the dark. This would do quite nicely. I took out my wallet and asked about ammunition. He said it would cost me another hundred. That was pretty steep for ammunition, but I wasn't about to argue with him. I handed him six hundred dollars and left.

I got up early the next morning and walked back into the woods. I found a place to fire my new gun. I had scrounged six beer bottles and set them about fifteen yards away. This would give me a good feel for the gun. I fired six shots in rapid succession and hit my target every time. I was pleased with myself—glad that I could still hit my target.

I went back into the resort for breakfast. I decided to try the same restaurant again, and I got the same sassy waitress as before. I ordered a Denver Omelet with hash browns and toast. When I had finished eating, I decided to try my hand at the poker table again. Luck wasn't with me this morning, so I left.

I handed out more flyers of Boris, but no luck there, either. I even drove to a few farms but was told the same thing. No one had seen Boris. *Was this trip another waste of my time?* Nothing was going right on this case, but I didn't want to admit defeat. I doubted if I would break even; I had too many unforeseen expenses. Although the taxpayers were footing the bill, I had to keep accurate records of every penny I spent. Keeping records wasn't my specialty. I had spent several thousand dollars and I doubted if I could come up with even half of the receipts. And the ones I did have were on the floors of my two cars. I hoped Tyler hadn't cleaned out my Mustang!

I grabbed an early dinner, and then went to my room to change into my dark clothes. Finally, it was getting dark. I drove past the farm where the bus had gone and pulled off the road as far as I could.

There was a small stand of trees between my car and the farm, so I had to pick my way carefully in the dark. It was too risky to go by the road and driveway. I walked toward the back of the property and hoped there weren't any dogs guarding the place. I had to climb over a wire fence and I was glad that I had remembered to pick up a pair of gloves at the store last night. The first building I came to was a wood shed. I opened the door slowly, not wanting to make to much noise. I shined the flashlight inside and saw just wood and woodcutting equipment—an ax, a couple of saws, and even a wood splitter. Old cobwebs hung eerily off the ceiling. It didn't look like anyone had been in this shed for a long time.

I closed the doors and looked around the farmyard. I saw a large white house that was greatly in need of repair; the white paint had long ago worn away leaving weather stains on the wood siding. The windows were partially open, and I saw the moon shining off the broken glass. There were a couple of shop buildings not far from the woodshed—one small building and a very large one. I was surprised how much was hidden back here. I would never have guessed there were so many buildings just by looking from the road. I chose the small one to search first. It was full of mechanic's tools. There were wrenches almost as big as I was. There was an old Model T that was actually in better condition then the old house. Someone had spent a lot of time on that old car. It kind of reminded me of the old cars that had been brought back to the Bronx two years ago. I moved on to the big metal shop. The shop was so large that it looked like an airplane hanger. There were no dogs in sight, so I peered into a small hole where a rivet was missing.

I was absolutely shocked by what I saw. A black spaceship of incredible size was sitting in the middle of the shed. It was circular with red and blue lights in the center. What was really strange was there were no windows. At least I couldn't see any even in the front.

There were three Morphs walking around the ship. Suddenly, a door opened and two men came out. They talked for a minute before one of them signaled to the ship. The spaceship lit up, a circle of colored lights bouncing off the wall. One of the Morphs drove a John Deere tractor onto a platform. They all put on some sort of weird glasses that had silver lenses and large black frames. One Morph then gave a "thumbs up" sign. Just as soon as he did that, an object on top of the space ship turned, aimed at the tractor, and shot a large red beam of light directly at it. The tractor was gone! The lights on the spaceship immediately went out and the three Morphs congratulated themselves. They walked up the ramp to the space ship and disappeared from sight.

I quit looking into the hanger and slid to the ground in amazement. I must have sat there for five minutes before I got my senses back. I wondered if all the Morphs on the bus were now in that spaceship. It certainly was large enough. Even so, this ship wasn't as large as the one I encountered in Massachusetts. *Maybe this was just a transport ship?* My question was soon answered. I heard a large rumbling sound come from up above. The ceiling of the hanger was pulled back. I saw my old friend, the mother ship, come into sight.

I definitely did not want to be seen, so I ran to a nearby woodpile. I looked up and saw the large spaceship was about a half-mile above me. I was amazed at how it could just suspend itself in midair.

The smaller ship rose straight up out of the hanger. It was soon inside the belly of the mother ship. Without any sound, they both disappeared. This had to be at the top of my list of strange cases.

CHAPTER EIGHTEEN

It was time for a serious change of plans. The following morning I went to the Sheriff's Office. In my line of work, you sometimes need to stretch the truth. Most of the time that is the only way to get someone to listen. I told the sheriff my story and said that I had gotten a tip that Boris was hiding at a nearby farm. I gave the sheriff the address of the farm that I was at last night. He was immediately interested in what I had to say. He knew that farm well. He had personally investigated the disappearance of the last renters that lived there. The elderly owners of the farm told him that they would drive out to the rental on the first of the month to collect their rent. They had been doing that for years; but this last time, no one was there. Every day for a week the farmer and his wife went back to the house, but no one was ever there. He became more and more worried, so he finally called the sheriff's office to investigate. A deputy was sent to check it out. Everything was left as if someone was still there. There was food in the refrigerator and clothes in the closet. No one had seen or heard a thing. After nine grueling months on the case, the sheriff filed it as unsolved.

The sheriff introduced himself as Sheriff Haskell. He had been the local sheriff for thirty years. I told him the story of my search for Boris, of all the miles I had traveled trying to catch him. I told him I was hoping this would be the end of the trail, as cowboys would say.

He listened thoughtfully, and then Sheriff Haskell assembled a team of six volunteers to go to the farm. He handed me a rifle. I hesitated for a second; I didn't like rifles. In my line of work, handguns were always better. You needed to be farther away from your target with a rifle. My targets always seemed to be up close and personal.

We headed out in three cars. The sheriff took the lead. He radioed in for an extra car with two more deputies. He wanted them to man the gate in case Boris tried to get away.

Sheriff Haskell drove slowly, giving the fourth car time to catch up. Five minutes later they were bringing up the rear. Haskell stopped well before the farmhouse to organize the group and fill them in on the plan. Once everyone and everything was in place, we headed in. The sheriff didn't waste any time. He drove as close to the house as possible, jumped out, and charged at the house. He had the front door kicked in before the rest of the team could even get out of their cars. They rushed in to find him standing inside smiling.

"Thought I would pump up your adrenaline," the sheriff laughed. I couldn't believe how quick he was.

Everyone split up into teams of two, searching the house for any signs that Boris had been there.

The house was still just the way the last tenants had left it. Pictures on the wall were crooked, clothes half folded, lying carelessly across a chair, and evidence of rats eating food left on the table long ago. Wallpaper was partially ripped from the wall, and the floor was starting to rot. I figured the roof must have been leaking. I wondered why the owner of the property didn't keep the house in any better repair. And why had it not been rented again? I realized it wasn't any of my business so I focused my attention on signs of Boris.

The sheriff walked into the room shaking his head at the disrepair. He told me the owners refused to rent the place until the case was solved.

I checked the upstairs. Being of a cautious nature, I carefully inspected a duffel bag I found hidden in one of the bedrooms. It contained a little over six thousand in cash, a change of clothes, and one of the flyers I had been passing out. I knew for certain then that the duffel bag belonged to Boris. I also found a receipt for ten thousand dollars from Plinks who owned the carnival.

After the deputies confirmed that Boris wasn't in the house, I showed Sheriff Haskell the contents of the duffel bag. He said he would have a few deputies watch the farm for a couple of days. With his getaway money here, Boris was bound to return for it.

Before we packed it in and returned to the station, the sheriff said he would personally check out all of the surrounding farms.

"Meanwhile, lets see what the boys have found in the sheds and other outbuildings," Sheriff Haskell said.

The smaller sheds just contained all of the maintenance tools and gadgets that you would expect to see on a working farm, though nothing looked like it had been used for many years. The sheriff and I then stepped into the hanger. The first thing we saw was the tractor that had disappeared earlier in front of my eyes. I checked out the spot where the flying saucer had been. Lying on the floor was some sort of plastic that looked like a windshield. It was very thin, no thicker than a strand of hair. I picked it up and bent it. It bounced right back to its original shape. I then folded it like a newspaper and the plastic bounced back again.

"Why I never..." the sheriff said. He was speechless.

He took the plastic from me. There was virtually no weight to it. Sheriff Haskell crumpled the plastic into a ball, a perfectly round ball. When he let go, the plastic once again returned to its original shape. He didn't know what to think. The sheriff admitted that he was puzzled; he had never seen such a thing.

He decided to have the plastic checked out by one of the science professors at the local college. He had used the professor several times as a consultant on some of his prior cases. It was a place to start.

Nothing else in the hanger was of any value to the case, so we left. The sheriff put four people in charge of watching the farm. There was obviously something odd about the happenings here.

"And if Boris returns, four men should be able to apprehend him, I reckon." Sheriff Haskell said. He considered his men exceptional and didn't have any reservations about leaving them alone on the farm.

The next four days were grueling. I canvased areas as far as Newport. No one had seen Boris. I had a strange feeling that Boris had been abducted by the Morph people, and that the young couple living there on the farm had been abducted, too. If that were true, it meant the Morphs had been here for years. I wasn't sure how to deal with that situation. It doesn't seem possible that of all the people in the world, I would be the first to see the Morphs. It just seemed too unlikely. *Were the governments around the world, aware of them*? Maybe the governments were, but didn't want a panic on their hands. I thought maybe the farm was a distribution area like big businesses use. Busses take the Morphs to a farm and the space ships distribute the people to other parts of the world. *Were these the children of the Morph people, ready to repopulate?*

I remembered Gramps words. "Things are picking up here." *Was Vermont the next place the Morphs were going?*

Were they planning to repopulate on Maggie's ranch? And if so, why? What was so important about her place? I knew the space ships had been working there already. She had no clue as she did not believe anything Gramps had told her. If Maggie had seen the spaceships, they would have made a fast detour to another state. Maggie wasn't the kind of gal you fooled with. If only she had believed Gramps.

Chapter Nineteen

Days went by with no sign of Boris. I was more and more sure that Boris had been captured by the Morphs. I decided to head back to Indiana until Sheriff Haskell was able to come up with new leads.

I got to the airport early and turned in my rental car. I was glad I was still wearing the necklace Pam and Sherry had given me. I hadn't ever seen so many Morphs in one place. My necklace was glowing a bright gold, and it wasn't going to go out any time soon, I thought. Not that many of them were traveling, but they were working in every area of the airport. They were in the food court, the bookstore, and even the liquor store. I wondered why so many were at the airport. Then as I boarded, I really got worried; my pilot was a Morph!

I hadn't bothered to call and let Nick know I was on my way back. Come to think of it, I hadn't bothered to call Nick at all since I had left. And it had been a while since I had called Maggie. I would call her later today, I promised myself.

I arrived at our house in the early morning. Nick was making breakfast when I walked in.

"Joe, Joe," Nick greeted me smiling. I shook his hand and said that I was happy to be back. While Nick finished making breakfast, I told him of my hunt for Boris. "It's been one goose chase after another," I lamented. "But it has been interesting," I added. Nick split the breakfast onto two plates and slid one plate over to me. He then poured two cups of coffee.

While we ate, Nick caught me up on what had been going here. He had been spending a lot of time in his store in South Bend. Steve had been home on leave from the Army, but not much else had happened.

"It's been pretty boring around here since you left, Joe," he said.

Nick asked me if I noticed anything different about the house.

"No," Joe replied with a grin. "I haven't been anywhere except the kitchen."

After we finished breakfast, I quickly did the dishes, as I was anxious to get to my room and take a much-needed shower. Just as I reached the stairs, Nick told me that Steve had left me a present on my dresser. I opened my bedroom door and saw a key and a note from Steve.

"Joe, here is the key to my room—check it out. I unlocked Steve's room and turned on the light. Straight ahead was another door. I opened it and found a slide. Not just any slide, but a tube slide— the kind you would find in an amusement park.

Nick walked up behind me.

"Wow!" I replied. "This is great." Nick pointed to the back of the note.

I turned it over and read it.

"Joe, enjoy your elevator ride to the cave." I was speechless—at least for now. I was sure I could come up with an idea that would outdo Steve's slide. *Just give me time*!

I spent the next couple of days relaxing and catching up on the chores that had been neglected since I'd been gone.

"Hey, Joe," Nick yelled up the stairs. "Let's try out Steve's slide."

I was game, so ten minutes later we met in Steve's room. Nick grabbed the sides of the slide and hoisted himself in. Seconds later, I was doing the same. The slide made twists and turns all the way to the top of the cave. I could hear Nick screaming. Then I soon knew why. It was a fifty-foot vertical drop from the ceiling of the cave to the water below.

"What a rush!" Nick yelled when my head popped out of the water. My heart was pounding so hard all I could do was nod my head. We swam back to the rocks that were at the edge of the water and climbed up.

"That deserves a second shot," Nick exclaimed.

I looked around and said, "We need to do something about this cave."

"What do you mean?" Nick asked.

"It needs to look more inviting, and we need an easier way to get back up those rocks."

Nick agreed. "We should lower a section of rocks and add some sand. We could have a small beach complete with tables and chairs!"

"Let's do it before Steve gets back home," I said.

Nick and I took a couple more trips down the slide, and then decided to go into Logansport. We took the elevator back up and got ready. I put on my necklace and remembered that I needed to give Nick his. I grabbed it and headed to the Camaro where he was waiting.

I was excited to be back in my own car and wanted to have a bit of fun. There was a long stretch of road and I put my Camaro through some quick maneuvers. I noticed Nick holding tighter to his seat and figured I should slow it down a bit. I saw some flashing lights come up behind me. I glanced at my speedometer and saw the red hand pointing to 90!

I pulled over and about two minutes later the cop came up to my car. I froze. The cop was a Morph. I kept my cool and told him that the Camaro was new, and I was just showing my friend what the car could do. The cop told me I was being reckless and the next time I was stopped, he would confiscate my car, new or not. He abruptly left without giving me a ticket.

Nick asked me why I was so nervous about the cop stopping me. I told him it was a long story, and I would tell him over dinner. As I held on to the necklace, I wondered if it was a curse or a blessing. I hadn't quite decided yet.

Both of us were quiet as we entered the bar. We were seated at a booth and ordered our drinks when the waitress came over. I told Nick that he was about to hear an unbelievable story.

The suspense was killing him. "Spill it, Joe," Nick said. But before I could speak, our drinks had arrived.

I wasn't quite sure how to tell him about the Morphs. It was a long, complicated story. But I knew Nick, and the best way to put it was straight.

"Nick," I said. "I saw aliens."

"What?" Nick questioned loudly. Several people in the bar looked over at us.

"Nick, keep your voice down. You never know who's listening," I said looking around a bit nervously.

I told him about Billy and the Mustang, the coin necklace from Pam and Sherry, and the mother ship and all the little spaceships at Maggie's. That brought the story to the present. When I told him about following the busload of Morph people, he understood why I was concerned about people overhearing our conversation. I ended with what I had seen at the farm.

Nick seemed calmer about all of this than I had expected, like he was trying to soak it all in. "I don't have any reason not to believe you, Joe—especially after all we have been through! The question is, what are you going to do about it?"

"I don't know yet," I said shaking my head helplessly. "I guess I was hoping you had some answers."

"Lets look at this logically," Nick said quietly. "You only see morph people when you wear your necklace, correct?

"Yes," I replied as I reached into my shirt pocket and handed a necklace to Nick. "Pam and Sherry told me to give this to you. I have another necklace for Steve."

Nick Picked up the necklace and slowly put it on. I explained how the necklace would glow a gold color whenever he saw a Morph. He nodded his head in understanding and mentioned that he could see the coin glowing when that cop stopped us earlier. He thought that it was just the sun shining on it.

Nick ordered another drink and asked who Maggie was. I told him how we met, but couldn't quite explain my relationship to her.

We finished our drinks and were heading to my car when two Morphs with machine guns shot at us from a black van. I saw the theater windows behind us exploding inwards. People were dropping to the floor. I didn't know if they had been shot or were just ducking for cover. Maybe both I thought. Nick instinctively grabbed me and tossed me into the

Camaro. The black van sped off around the corner.

Blood dripped from Nick's forehead. I quickly maneuvered my body into a driving position.

"That was close," Nick muttered breathlessly as he climbed in.

"I recognized those two Morphs," I told Nick. "They were in the booth behind us in the bar.

Did a bullet nick you?" I asked.

"No, I cut my forehead on the corner of the car door when I shoved you in," Nick said.

"I think we should spend the night in town," I suggested.

"Probably so, Joe," Nick answered quietly.

We drove around for a few hours trying to find the black van, but we didn't have any luck.

We drove back by the bar on our way to find a motel. There were still cops on the scene at the theatre. Witnesses were eagerly telling their stories. Things like that didn't happen every day, at least around here. Nick had his window down and heard the cops say how lucky people were because only four were wounded, no one seriously.

"That's good news," I breathed.

"You bet," he replied. I wouldn't want anyone hurt because of us."

We went to the Captain Logan Hotel and got a couple of rooms. I was tired, so I took the elevator to the top floor where my room was, while Nick climbed the stairs to his second floor room.

I headed to the coffee shop as soon as I woke up but Nick was already there.

"How's the forehead?" I asked him.

"Fine, more bruised than cut," Nick said, patting his wound.

Nick asked if there were a lot of Morphs in Logansport. We finished our third cup of coffee and decided to find out. Nick wanted to test out his necklace, so we drove to a busy street corner and parked. We stepped out of the car and walked toward the bench under the People's Drug Store awning. It didn't take long for our necklaces to begin glowing.

I sensed Nick stiffen. "Are you ok, Nick?"

He was in shock. The man walking past him was just as I had described.

"I'm ok." Nick said, "Check this guy out." I did. I was almost desensitized by the Morphs by now.

"We need to do something about them," Nick whispered.

"I agree, but what can we do?" I asked.

"I'm not sure, yet," Nick replied.

We sat on the bench for an hour counting as many as they could. It was about one Morph to fifty humans.

"That's a lot, Nick said.

I was thinking the same thing.

Nick wanted to go to the authorities, but I was against it for now. What if just one Morph was working at the police station? If the Morphs found out we knew, we would be in big trouble. We were already on their radar.

I touched my jaw and told Nick about what happened to one of my molars and my narrow escape.

"Ouch!" Nick said. "I can't even imagine what that must have been like. I sure don't want to go through anything like that."

I wasn't about to go through that again, either, so we

needed to something—and quick!

"I have a meeting in Washington D.C. in a few days, Nick. I have to go over the details of the Boris case. It's going to be an exhausting meeting. I'm going to have to watch what I say and to whom I say it. I can't mention Maggie or the Morphs. And I have to justify all of these expenses—and I did spend a lot."

"I'm not sure who we can talk to in D.C. about the Morph situation. You should be there, too, Nick," I said. "You've experienced them firsthand."

"I won't be able to add much, but it sure would be interesting," he added thoughtfully.

Nick and I went back home and just relaxed the rest of the day. We took a few more slides down to the cave before going to bed. We were like a couple of kids.

CHAPTER TWENTY

The next morning I was having coffee when Nick came into the kitchen.

"Good morning, Joe."

"Morning, Nick," I mumbled. I didn't sleep much. Between worrying about Maggie, the Morphs, and my expense account, I couldn't relax enough to drop off for more than an hour at a time.

"Hey, Joe, what do you think the Morphs want?"

"I'm not sure," I replied. "But they must want something we have pretty bad." I handed Nick a fresh cup of coffee and walked out of the room saying I needed to give Maggie a call. I searched my pocket for her phone number, thinking I should have it memorized by now. I fished out a half-wadded up piece of paper with her number barely legible. She answered the phone on the first ring.

"Hello," Maggie said.

"Hi Maggie," I said softly.

"Oh, Joe! I'm so glad you called." Maggie quickly broke down. "Something terrible has happened here."

"What's wrong, Maggie?" I asked.

"It's Gramps. He disappeared two days ago, Joe. Sometimes he isn't in his right mind. Gramps is lost somewhere. We found his truck over by the ridge. Oh Joe, I'm so worried about him," Maggie cried.

I hated what was going through my mind. I was more than half afraid that Gramps had been abducted by the Morphs.

"I'm sorry, Maggie. Is there anything I can do?" I asked gently.

"I wish there was something you could do. The whole town is hunting for him. They even brought out the search dogs, but no luck. I wish you were here," Maggie replied with regret in her voice. "But I can't think about anything except finding Gramps."

"I'm really sorry, Maggie. Call me when you find him."

"It was good to hear your voice, Joe."

I told Nick about Gramps' disappearance and said that Maggie thought it best if I wasn't there.

Nick said he was sorry to hear that, and if he could be of any help to just say the word. He also said he needed to leave for a few hours, but didn't say where he was going. I said that I had errands to run, anyway. Among other things, I needed to get an oil change. Nick suggested we switch cars because he was meeting a friend at a nearby service station, so he could take care of the oil change for me.

Nick and I were both going into Logansport, but this time he was driving the Camaro and I was folded awkwardly in the VW Bug. I wasn't sure what he saw in this little tin can, but he loved it. I was sure that somebody, somewhere, someday, would be burying Nick in this car.

While I was in town, I decided to check out a couple of handmade tables for the cave. I saw an ad in the Tribune and decided to take a look.

I found the house. The yard was full of handmade outdoor furniture. The tables were great. There were several sets of tables and chairs with beach themes. *Perfect.* I was impressed with the workmanship, so I ordered two tables and eight chairs with a promise of delivery the next day.

I finished all of my errands and was on my way home when I saw my Camaro on the side of the road. I stopped, but Nick was nowhere to be seen. I checked inside the car and saw the keys. I turned the ignition and it started up just fine. I had just switched off the engine when I heard a scream coming from an old deserted house nearby.

I quietly went to the old house and tiptoed to one of the windows, but I didn't see anything except dirty floors, a floor lamp with no shades, and an old clock sitting on top of the fireplace mantel.

I didn't hear any more screams or see anyone or anything that could have made that sound, so I wondered if it was just my imagination or a wild animal.

The house was obviously abandoned, so I decided to go inside. The front door was unlocked. As I entered, I couldn't help but wish I had my gun. It wasn't doing me any good sitting in my room on the dresser top!

I walked into the room I had seen from the window. I stepped carefully around the broken bits of glass and got a closer look at the fireplace. I noticed that it was ajar. I pulled on it and moved it enough to peer behind it. It was one of those fake fireplaces that anyone could buy for fifty bucks at any furniture store.

I ran back out and got a flashlight out of the Camaro glove box. I shined the flashlight behind the fireplace. There was a crooked stairway leading down. I had seen so many secret passages these past two years that I was no longer surprised by anything. I needed to go in to find Nick, but it looked pretty tight. I could barely squeeze my large frame behind it, but I managed. I carefully stepped down the stairs and ended up in a basement. It was very small. There was a water heater standing alone in one corner and a shelf full of rusted tools in another. There was a dim light peeking through the cracks of the wall behind the tools, so I slid the tool shelf back. It was on wheels, so it moved easily. I was in a wide tunnel. I was having second thoughts about going any farther, but my concern about Nick made me continue.

I followed the tunnel for about a mile. Surprisingly, there were small hills going up and down. I had never seen anything like it. I pushed cobweb after cobweb out of my way. *I hate spiders.* I was hoping these webs were as ancient as the house.

I tripped on something and shined my light down at the floor of the tunnel. It was a body, and I jumped back against the tunnel wall. I shined the flashlight farther up the tunnel and saw a graveyard of human bones. The bones were still clothed—all had on the same type of outfits. Some outfits were shorter so I could only imagine that they were women. The clothes resembled the kind you would wear on a safari. Some were still wearing glasses, lying crooked on their faces, and most of the skeletons still had rings on their fingers. One body was lying on its stomach. I could see something in the back pocket. I took out a wallet and checked it for identification. The wallet contained thirty-three dollars and a driver's license. The man's name was Orval Beck. He would be about 50 years old now. The license showed his birth date as 1920.

I put the wallet in my pocket and continued farther into the tunnel. It was getting colder and damper. It felt as though I had gone deeper into the earth. The tunnel zigzagged, and as I looked down, I could see the paths I had been on earlier. I soon arrived at a room that had been excavated. I could see old rotted strings tied to posts. There were a lot of holes in the ground with numbered markers inside them. I wondered what they were digging for. *Dinosaurs?* I laughed a bit nervously. I moved on through the tunnel and found small wooden boxes in another room. They were partially filled with bones. I didn't think they were big enough to be dinosaur bones. They looked like human bones. If I remembered my anatomy right, the bones were a little off. These were not human bones. *Morph bones?*

I moved on down the tunnel and found another room. This room had commercial, walk-in type refrigerators. I stepped inside and found big tube-like jars with strange body parts. One jar had claw-like hands in it. Another contained what looked like a heart that was twice the size of a human's. I saw eyes staring at me from a tall glass jar and there were small legs in another. What was even scarier were the black permanent marker lines drawn on the side of the jar showing how much the legs had grown. I was getting freaked out, so I decided to hightail it out of the refrigerator.

I was concerned about Nick and wasn't sure if I should go back and look around outside or continue on through this tunnel hoping I would find him here. I didn't see evidence of him in the house or the tunnel so decided that I should just move on as quickly as I could. I ended up in another room where there were metal skeletons in the shape of human beings. I was shocked beyond words—skin had started to grow on the metal skeletons!

Then it hit me—they had been making monsters out of metal! They used their homegrown organs to put inside the metal so "it" would function like a human. *This was Frankenstein all over again.*

I picked up a scrap of the metal and noticed it was the same metal my necklace was made from. I remembered Pam and Sherry's words: "The necklace is made from a metal not of earth."

Just then, I was hit from behind. I woke up in a room with nothing but the bed that I was lying in. I wasn't tied up, which surprised me. I soon understood why. The room had metal bars like a jail, and I could see that I was locked in. There was a metal door leading to another room. The door was open. I quietly got up from my bed to check out the other room. There was a toilet, a writing desk, and one chair. I sat down at the desk found a pen and writing paper. There were two small drawers. I opened one and found a journal from Orval Beck.

CHAPTER TWENTY-ONE

Orval Beck wrote that during WWII, there seemed to be some activity in his squadron that defied logic. Germans were firing at them from behind enemy lines. Orval's men fired back. This back and forth lasted through the night. By morning, there seemed to be a cease-fire on the German side.

"My men hoped it was because the Germans were low on ammo," he wrote. "We cautiously slipped to the German side. We met no resistance from them. As we entered their compound, we found the reason for the cease-fire. The Germans were all dead.

"Some had been sleeping, some eating, some lying on the ground with weapons still in their hands. They all had one thing in common—they had been shot, but by something other then our weapons.

"It was as if they had been shot by some kind of weapon that made no sound. We hadn't heard any firing at all from that side of the line. Every soldier had a hole in his body that had been cauterized. No blood had even dripped onto their uniforms. It was like some force outside of this world was helping us. We had heard of similar reports by other Allied outfits. Japanese submarines were being destroyed as the Navy just stood by and watched."

The journal went on to say that Orval had seen secret documents where U.S. pilots testified that they had seen spaceships. These spacecraft had outmaneuvered and outrun their own planes so they couldn't get close enough to see who was flying them. Men in the infantry had seen these ships and were told by the government never to speak a word of it. The government was developing a secret investigation into these reports, as there were too many similar reports to discount.

One last entry in the diary mentioned that there was a midnight crash of a foreign object by a lake just outside Logansport, Indiana. Orval continued, "It occurred just after the war. It was kept top secret until one day I got a call from a man claiming to work for the government. I was to meet him at Riverside Park in Logansport, Indiana, on August seventh at nine a.m. He would be wearing a white carnation in his jacket and would wait on a bench near the merry-go-round.

"I was asked to head up a team of archaeologists. We were to go to a deserted house outside Logansport where there was believed to be an old gravesite of aliens. I was instructed to keep this expedition quiet. I was to report my findings to him and only to him. We had only been there for a day when the same species of alien came back to the house and killed my team.

"They not only killed them, but tortured them as well. I'm the only surviving member. My time will soon be up, I fear. There is no hope." That final entry was for Valentine's Day, February 14, 1947.

Wow! I was in disbelief. What a journal. I put it in my pocket along with Beck's wallet. I wondered why it was left in the room for me to find. I began to wonder if I would be making out my own journal. *And who would come after me to read it?* I looked at my watch; I had been held in this cell for over three hours now.

I went back into the previous room and stretched out on the bed. I needed to think. I had gotten myself out of some strange situations, but this one had become the most hopeless. I stared at the ceiling and could see drawings that were probably made by previous prisoners. The drawings made no sense. One was of a brick, another of a door. A third was of the cell I was in.

I must have fallen asleep because I had a dream that I was tied to a post and tortured by monsters of every kind. I was suddenly awakened by a Morph bringing me food. He never said a word. He slid the tray under the doorjamb along with a flattened out water canteen. Then he was gone. I yelled for "him" to come back, but he ignored me. As I sat on the bed wondering if it was safe to eat, I realized that this was my third nightmare—two of them this year. I had to figure a way out of here.

I paced back and forth like a helpless, expectant father. I shook the bars and hoped they would give way, but no luck. I even spent the rest of the evening trying to find a hidden door. It was damp and chilly down here, so I grabbed my blanket. It was thin, but it would help. The cave walls were starting to mentally close in on me. *Would I be the next one drawing strange things on the ceiling?* As I lay on the bed looking at the drawing of the brick, I had to wonder how they even got up there. The ceiling, even standing on the bed, was at least another three feet above my head. Even if you used the desk chair in the other room, it didn't seem possible. Besides, it would be too wobbly. It was after midnight now, so I decided to get some rest. I wanted to be alert when the Morph came back. Maybe I would have a chance to rip out his throat.

I awoke from a deep sleep by the sound of screams coming from somewhere close by. All I could think of was my molar that had been pulled. It was seven in the morning and the screams were getting louder. I listened carefully to see if I could tell which direction the sounds were coming from. It was Nick! I knew his voice. I yelled out, but no answer. The screams lasted for another fifteen minutes before the silence came. I kept calling his name, but he didn't respond. I paced back and forth calling Nick's name every five minutes. I needed to keep my adrenaline high. That was the only advantage I had. I started shadow boxing and hoped one of the Morphs would dare come in.

As I started to do pushups, a Morph brought me breakfast. "Give me your tray," he demanded. As I slid the tray underneath the bars, he slid my food and water back under.

I asked him why I was being held, but he didn't respond. He just walked away. It was about noon, so I figured I had been here for almost a full day. I sat with my elbows on the table, desperate to come up with a plan. I must have sat there for a good five minutes before I heard a faint sound echoing through the tunnel. It was Nick.

"Joe, are you there?"

"Yes, Nick, are you okay?" I asked back.

"I'm not doing very good, Joe. They beat me pretty badly and pulled out one of my fingernails yesterday. They wanted to know where I got the necklace. But I didn't give in. I don't know how much longer I can last. They said they were coming back for a repeat performance tomorrow."

"Hold on for as long as you can, Nick. It's the only way. I'll get us out of here, I promise."

"Hurry, Joe," Nick responded faintly. Then he was silent. I hoped he had passed out to get some relief from the pain.

I had to find a way. Knowing Nick was in for more punishment gave me the strength I needed to do something—anything! I looked in the other desk drawer. There was a hand drawn map of the cave starting from the fireplace in the old house. It showed the tunnel and all the rooms off of it, even my cell. At least now I had a place to start. I looked closer at the map and saw where the other tunnels led. There was a tunnel on both sides of my cell. But when I was looking for a way out, the backside of my cell seemed to be nothing but hard rock. There was no secret door, I was positive of that. I'd had plenty of experience looking for secret doors these last two years.

I leaned back in my chair and looked again at the drawings on the ceiling. One was of a bridge leading off in two separate directions. One way went to another cell. The other led to a stairway. Someone must have been held captive for a long time to be able to make such detailed drawings on the ceiling. I was still puzzled as to how they even got up there.

Once again, it was mealtime. I was getting the hang of this routine, switching out one tray for another. Neither one of us said a word.

Nick's voice once again came echoing through the tunnels. "Joe, are you still there?"

"Yes, Nick, I'm here."

"Joe, I have drawings on my ceiling." he said.

"What are the drawings of, Nick?" I yelled.

"One is of a stairway leading down into what looks like a missile silo."

"What's the other one of?" I asked hoping the conversation would keep his mind off of his pain.

"There's a set of stairs leading into a cornfield."

"Nick, are you able to walk?" I asked.

" I think so. Why?"

"Are you in a cell?"

"Yes, a two room cell," Nick replied slowly, obviously getting weaker.

"Are there any drawings in the other room?" I asked, my mind trying to make sense of it all.

"Let me check. It'll take me a bit to get there. I don't have much strength left." After a minute, he barely got out the details. "It's of an upside down table."

"Are there any tables in your cell, Nick?" I asked, hardly allowing myself to hope.

"Yes, there's one table and a chair."

Now I thought I understood what the drawings were for. They were clues showing how to escape the cell.

I turned my desk upside down, and a round metal door stared me in the face, but there was no way to open it. There wasn't a handle and there didn't seem to be any way could I pry it open. I sat trying everything I could to get it open when I heard the Morph coming back. *Had it been that long since lunch?* No, he just needed my tray. I was grateful he couldn't see into this second room. I bent down to slide the tray underneath the door. Then I saw it—the brick that was in the drawing. *Why hadn't I seen it before?* I waited for the Morph to leave. I pulled the brick toward me. I could hear the sound of a spring connecting and the grinding sound of metal. I walked back into the second room and the metal door was upright. There were stairs leading downwards

I told Nick what I had found and said he had to do the same thing. He would have to wait until after supper so we had more time. I was pretty sure once the morph people brought supper, they wouldn't come back again until morning. I put the door back down and waited.

Normally, it seemed that one meal came on top of another. But now, time seemed to drag. It was finally dinnertime. As usual, the Morph slipped dinner under the door and left without saying a word. I quickly moved the desk and pulled back on the brick. Without a second thought, I ran down the stairs. Nick soon joined me, barely able to walk. His fingertip looked like a bloody stub and his face was cut and bruised from being repeatedly hit.

"Joe, my ribs were beaten pretty badly. I can walk but not fast."

"I know, Nick. We'll take it as slow as we can."

We weren't sure which direction to go in the tunnel. In my haste to escape, I forgot to bring the map. We couldn't escape without it, so I climbed back up into my cell to get it.

"Close the lid, Joe," Nick said.

"What?" I asked.

"Close the lid so the table will right itself. That way the Morphs won't know how we got out."

I closed the lid and heard the table move and fall back into place. He's is going to be ok, I thought.

I looked at the map and decided that we needed to head east, which would be to the left if my back was against the cell door.

"This way, friend," I said pointing east with my finger.

After a lot of walking through the tunnel, we came to the bridge. I looked down and could tell that it was a long way to the bottom.

"Look down there, Nick," I said.

He looked down, then picked up a rock and dropped it. A Morph standing below heard it hit bottom and asked what that noise was.

We saw two morph people look at the rock that had fallen.

"It's just a rock," one of them said looking up at the bridge.

We were bent low now with only our eyes showing.

"I'm surprised that as old as this cave is, we don't have more rocks falling." Satisfied, they left.

We crossed the bridge and found two different paths leading in opposite directions. One went to the left and one to the right.

"I think the left goes to the missile silo," I said to Nick. "The right one goes to another cell. So I guess we go left."

"No, Joe. What if someone else is in that cell? We can't just leave them."

"Okay. To the right it is." I headed into the right tunnel and in five minutes, we were at the cell. What we saw surprised us both. We found a skinny old man with a beard down to his knees.

"Mister," I whispered.

The old man slowly lifted his head and asked, "Who are you?"

"My name is Joe and this is my friend, Nick."

"How did you find me?" he asked with a quivering

voice.

"We were also held captive but managed to escape," Nick said. "We're going to help you get out of here."

Nick told the old man what to do while I stood watch. He did as Nick directed and pulled the brick toward himself. This time, instead of a door opening under the desk, the cell door popped open.

"Well, I'll be," the old man said. If you two only knew how many times I stubbed my toe on that there old brick." We looked down at his feet and saw that he was barefooted.

"We had better get out of here before someone comes," I said.

The old man grabbed some papers and shoved them into his pocket. We closed the cell door and headed east again. In no time, we passed the bridge, and after going through a series of ups and downs and winding tunnels, we came to some stairs leading up. The three of us climbed the stairs, Nick and the old man barely making it. There was a door just above our heads. It was more of a hatch, like you would find in a submarine. I tried turning it, but it wouldn't budge. Nick tried to help. Between the two of us, the hatch soon gave way. We climbed up into a room full of big computers. There were two chairs in front of them. We could tell this missile site had only recently been abandoned. Maybe only months ago, as the papers on the desk were dated this year.

There were Army rations and a couple more rooms with beds.

"Look at this," I said going over to a rifle cabinet.

"These will come in handy," Nick said smiling now. We each grabbed an M-14. There was plenty of ammunition, so we loaded the rifles and packed our pockets with as much ammo as we could.

The old man, however, was more interested in the rations than the weapons. In one of the rooms, we found a ladder positioned against a wall. Against my better judgment, Nick decided to climb up the ladder. I thought he was still too weak.

Once at the top, he yelled that there were buttons you had to press to get out—like on a keypad.

The old man continued eating his rations, but now he was looking at the manuals. "Six, five, seven, twelve," shouted the old man, looking up at Nick.

Nick immediately caught on and asked him to repeat the numbers. The old man did, and Nick pressed them in sequence. There was the sound of air pressure being released and the hatch opened up.

We saw daylight for the first time in two days.

I smiled with gratitude at the old man. He pushed me away with a wave of his hand and told me that it was just kid stuff. I helped him up the ladder where we stood in the middle of a cornfield. The corn was above our heads, and we weren't sure which way to go. We heard voices that sounded as if they weren't too far away. I could see a Morph heading right toward us.

"Here they are, he yelled to his companions. I could see at least five Morphs running our way. I yelled for Nick to watch out as I aimed my M-14 down the row where they were running. Three went down, but the other two turned into the next row where Nick was. They began shooting back. Instead of bullets, though, rays of light shot past me, disintegrating the corn stalks one by one. Somehow my M-14 didn't seem quite so powerful.

Nick stepped out from behind a stalk, aimed his rifle at a Morph and fired. He flinched as he put his finger on the trigger and began yelling that this was the one who pulled out his fingernail. Then Nick fired one more shot killing the last Morph.

We were almost out of the cornfield when we heard the sound of at least a dozen more Morphs headed our way. Nick shouted that one of them was the sheriff who had stopped him in the Camaro on his way home. We looked at the old man and asked him if he had any ideas. He looked up from his pack of cheese crackers and nodded his head. The old man, not saying a word, waited for the Morphs to get closer. With a finger on his mouth, he signaled for us to be very still and quiet.

As soon as they got close enough, he ran straight toward them and tossed grenades in their direction.

One explosion after the other sent Morph body parts flying into the cornfield. Only one Morph was left. He charged the old man, his arms stretched out and his hands in a fist. It was the angriest look I had ever seen. As the Morph came within arms length of the old man, he went down. Nick had put a bullet clean through the Morph's temple. His look of thanks said more than words could have.

We rushed over to the old man to ask him what the heck he thought he was doing, taking on a dozen Morphs all alone.

The old mam replied, "I always was a bit of a showman." We had a good laugh and then searched for our car.

As we were walking, the old man said that while we were playing with our rifles, he had found the grenades next to the rations. He figured they might come in handy!

CHAPTER TWENTY-TWO

It was after midnight by the time we found our cars.

"You're coming home with us for the night," Nick told the old man.

"Fine with me," he replied. "I just don't want to put you guys out. Truth is, I don't have anywhere else to go at the moment."

We were exhausted by the time we got home. The tables and chairs had been delivered and were sitting on the front porch. We moved them out of the way and would deal with them later.

We went in and I made us all a quick cheese omelet. I tossed in a few extra eggs because I had seen how much the old man could pack away. Nick was young and just naturally ate a lot. His injuries didn't affect his appetite, but I did notice he handled his fork with special care. We were all pretty quiet while we ate.

The old man had some adjusting to do, and Nick was in pain. Getting out of that tunnel alive took its toll on Nick. I had a new respect for him after seeing how he kept going after all he had just been through.

We were all exhausted, but we still had some questions for the old man, but that could wait until tomorrow. He slept in Nick's room.

I slept in later than normal. I peeked into Steve's room to check on Nick, but he was already up. It was after 8:00 before I finally got downstairs. Nick was already gone.

The old man was sitting at the counter drinking a cup of black coffee and reading the newspaper. He said he had not seen a real paper in many years. He was actually enjoying himself. I'm not sure he even knew who was president.

Just as I asked him what he would like for breakfast, Nick came in with a shopping bag and two women friends of his.

"Jodie and Maoris, meet Joe," introduced Nick. Nick said that Jodie was a barber and Maoris was a stylist. They were here to make the old man look like new again.

Nick introduced the old man to the girls, and after a quick bowl of oatmeal, they all went up to Nick's room to give the old man a makeover.

Two hours later, the old man, followed by the two girls, came back out of Nick's room.

"Pretty impressive," Joe said to the old man. His beard was gone, and he was wearing the new clothes Nick had bought.

After the girls left, the three of us sat at the kitchen table and finished off the pot of coffee. Nick and I told the old man a bit about ourselves—our jobs, how we met, and how we came to be at the old house outside of Logansport.

Now it was his turn.

"First of all, my name is Orval Beck."

"Why that can't be true," I hollered out. "I saw Orval Beck's body in the graveyard under the house."

I quickly ran upstairs to my room and retrieved Orval Beck's wallet and journal. I left the journal on the entry table, but handed the wallet to the old man who looked at it a bit sadly, as if remembering.

"No," Orval said, "you saw a body. The Morphs weren't concerned about who wore what clothes.

"Sometimes they would experiment on two or three of us at a time. When they were finished with us, they just grabbed any clothing and put it on us. We were all subjected to abominable experiments. Most eventually ended in death, but for some reason they wanted to keep me alive."

He opened the buttons on his new shirt and showed us the scars running down his body. Nick and I were shocked to speechlessness that a human body could endure such cruelty and live, let alone still be sane.

"Anyway," Orval said, "They were trying to put a metal body together using human body parts. Most of the bodies you passed had internal organs missing. I was kept alive only in case they needed more parts. Why they chose me, I'm not certain. Years went by and as Morphs came and went, I was just kind of forgotten. They started out taking decent care of me. I got fed three times a day like clockwork. Eventually, I got fed only once a day, if they remembered. I got to the point where I would stockpile half the food I was given just in case I was totally forgotten. I learned to get by on very little. Suddenly I started getting regular meals again. It must have been because you two had been brought in.

"Do you boys mind if I use your phone?" Orval asked suddenly.

"No, go ahead. It's in the den right off the entryway,"

Joe said.

Orval excused himself and stepped out to use the phone. A couple of minutes later, he was back saying the numbers he had didn't work.

I looked at the phone numbers Orval had, and explained that phone numbers now had more digits in them. I showed him how to use directory assistance.

About thirty minutes later, Orval came back into the kitchen with the news that someone from the Pentagon's local office in Indianapolis was coming to pick him up. They would be here in about an hour.

"Orval, I found this in my cell," I said, handing him his journal.

"Thanks, Joe. I used to be moved from cell to cell and wondered where I had left it," Orval said.

We continued talking about the journal until we heard a knock on the door. Two uniformed men had arrived to pick him up. A few minutes later we said goodbye to him. I hoped we would see him again.

I decided to call Maggie to see if they had found Gramps. I was hesitant because I didn't want to be a distraction to her, yet I wanted to be there if she needed me.

The voice that answered was not Maggie's.

"May I speak to Maggie, please?" I asked the unknown voice.

"This is Agent Graham of the F. B. I. To whom am I speaking?"

I gave him my name and explained that I was a close friend. I was just calling to see if her grandfather had been found. Agent Graham informed me that not only had Gramps disappeared, but Maggie and all her help were gone, too. "Nine people are missing, Mr. Craig. Two of the people are Saudi citizens, and you know what international implications that can have. Any information you have would be most appreciated."

I told Agent Graham that I had to be in Washington D.C. in two days. I could be at the farm after that. After a few personal questions, Graham said he would see me in a couple of days.

I went back into the kitchen where Nick was finishing up dishes.

"Maggie and everyone on the ranch has disappeared, Nick, and I think the Morphs took them."

Zorko put down Joe's journal and sat thinking for a moment. He was very pleased with himself. Maggie was a great find. He knew when Gramps was getting vocal about his spaceship sightings that it was time to take Maggie to Sagitar. He was sure she would be a fighter, but once there, she would be smart enough to see what a good life she would have. Everything she needed would be there for her. His only concern was what to do with these earthly emotions called love. He was seeing that it was almost a necessity. Maggie needed Joe. He picked up Maggie's journal and reread the part about her capture. He didn't like to think about her being distressed. Such emotions could destroy a person. He needed Maggie to be the strong person he had seen in years past. Her value depended on it.

I couldn't move. It was dark. Had I been in a wreck? No, I hadn't been driving. Had I fallen off my horse? Now I remembered. I had been waiting by the phone for information about Gramps. Where was I? I could hear people talking. I kept hearing a thud over and over again. It sounded strangely like books being put on a shelf.

Hours passed and the light of morning brought more questions. When I awoke, a young giant of a girl was holding me in her hands. I knew then that I had to be dreaming. She sat me on a table, picked up a brush, and smoothed out my hair. The little girl turned me around to admire her handiwork. I saw a giant boy playing with an action figure that was waving its hands and yelling for help.

He stuck out his tongue and tormented the little girl by saying, "My toy is better than your stupid doll. Yours doesn't move or talk."

The little girl continued brushing my hair.

"Now your hair is much better," she cooed at me. She then patted my head and put me in a little house. I realized then that the children weren't giants, but that I was tiny. I couldn't quite tell, but I suspected I was only five or six inches tall. Somehow I had been shrunken and was now living in a dollhouse.

Beautiful, sparkling chandeliers hung from the ceiling. A white, plush carpet covered the floor. Stuffed animals surrounded cozy brown chairs and a fireplace. I walked into the next room and found two staircases, one on each side of the room. I climbed up them and found three furnished bedrooms. I opened a dresser drawer and found it stuffed with girls' clothes. I looked in the closet; it was filled with beautiful dresses. There were blue dresses, flowered dresses, and white laced designer dresses. There was even a white chiffon wedding dress.

I walked up one more flight of stairs that led to the roof. When I looked down, I could see an expensive car in the driveway, an apple tree laden with ready to pick fruit, and a perfectly manicured yard. I heard a giggle, looked up, and a pair of gigantic hands reached down and grabbed me.

The young girl had me again and was shaking me, telling me that I was boring. I kept shaking my head back and forth, trying to wake up from this nightmare, but it was useless; the dream just wouldn't go away.

The young girl, disappointed, put me back on what looked like a bookshelf. Everything was dark again. Then I heard that thud, thud, thud again.

Above the thudding noise, I heard the little girl crying, "I want a princess to play with," and the words "Princess, princess, where are you?"

Soon the girl's voice stopped. I heard footsteps, heavy footsteps, coming close to me. Daylight again. An ugly, ugly, man was holding me in his hands. He was flipping through pages in a book.

Then looking at me, the ugly man said, "Yes, Maggie, you're the one."

A woman's voice said, "Will that be all, Zorko?"

"Yes, that's it," Zorko said as he swung me back and forth as if testing me out before setting me on a counter.

The lady, obviously a store clerk of some kind, picked me up. I could hear a beep, beep, and then she said, "Zorko, do you need food for Maggie? We have a month's supply for fifty pieces."

"Oh, yes, please," Zorko answered and handed her ten thousand fifty pieces.

When will this nightmare be over? I must have fainted because I woke up lying against a mound of hay. My stallion stood next to me eating. I was in my barn; the nightmare was finally over.

"I never want to go through that again," I said, looking at my horse. I stood up and hugged him, wondering if the police had called yet about Gramps.

I left the barn and headed to the house. Tyler was walking toward me and I called out to him, so happy to see a familiar face.

"Tyler!"

"Yes, Miss Maggie?"

"Tyler, I just had the most awful nightmare." I told him what I had dreamed. Just telling the story was enough to send shivers of fear through my body. After I was finished about my nightmare, he spoke softly.

"Miss Maggie, I had almost the identical dream. Isn't that just a bit strange?"

"Has anyone found Gramps, yet?" I asked Tyler.

"Yes," Tyler responded. "Your Gramps, he just showed back up at the house like nothing ever happened."

"'Gramps! Gramps!' I rushed toward the house.

"The front door opened and he walked out. I gave him the biggest hug and asked him where he had been. After I told him my dream, he said that he, too, had had a similar dream.

"I just didn't know what to think. Gramps interrupted her thoughts and said someone needed to get to town and buy supplies. The pantry and refrigerator were empty and the horses and other animals were low on feed.

"I could take the truck and go shopping for food and farm supplies later today. First, though, I wanted to call Joe to tell him that Gramps was all right. I tried several times, but there was no dial tone. Gramps told me it hadn't worked all day. I decided to stop by the phone company on my way into town.

"I had only driven about fifty feet out of our driveway when the sky in front of me got dark. I thought it strange because the sun was still out and there were only a few wispy clouds. I got out of the car and walked about two feet and bumped into a wall. I scratched at the wall and black paper filled my hands.

"Zorko of my "dream" was looking in at me smiling. I let out a thunderous scream.

"Don't scream," Zorko admonished.

"He picked me up, and I could see we were in a very large room with fake sun and clouds. He began talking to me, explaining that I was unique, that I made his set complete. Zorko said he had gotten my entire life from the book. He already had the horses, Gramps, Tyler, and the guests from Saudi Arabia. He now owned everyone and everything that was in the book of Maggie.

"I could only listen. As Zorko talked, he half petted, half caressed me. He told me the only other person on his planet to have a complete set was the High

Commander.

"A complete set of books demands a lot of money and honor on this planet," Zorko told me matter-of-factly.

"While he was talking, I was trying to figure a way out. First, though, he would have to set me down. Zorko continued telling me stories about the High Commander. He told me that the HC was on earth during the end of WWII. He was in Germany and had personally captured Hitler, some of his henchmen, and many townspeople.

"'Just like you, they are all here. And just like you, they are all small. You will all have a good, long life; here, you can expect to live at least two thousand years.

"The HC built Hitler and his people a five-mile city. They grow their own food, make their own clothes, and essentially live a carefree life. And once in a while, Hitler will even give a speech. He will raise his fist at the HC and threaten to someday take over the planet. He tells all of his people they were the superior race once and they can be again. They need to prepare to battle those that hold them captive. Ha! Maybe he will; he has already gathered an army of ten thousand.

"The High Commander created someone else to look just like Hitler and left him on earth to take his place. Your whole world believes Hitler is dead; but he's alive and well, right here on our planet.'"

Zorko took another book from the shelf. Maggie could see it was titled Kitti.

"'No, not my sister!" Maggie cried.

"Zorko gently put Kitti and her kids with Maggie. Maggie and Kitti hugged tightly

"She whispered to Kitti that Zorko was bragging he had a complete set and that we were very valuable. But he doesn't know about Schotzie. He really doesn't have a complete set, yet. "Kitti was confused and crying. I was sure she hadn't really heard what I was trying to tell her.

"I didn't know how to tell Gramps and Tyler they were being taken to another planet. It would kill Gramps when he found out. He is so independent. And what about the buyers from Saudi Arabia? I couldn't make myself tell any of them what had happened. I guessed they would find out soon enough."

Satisfied that Maggie would settle in well and

be of great value, Zorko set down her journal and continued to read more about Joe.

"I'm sorry to hear that. I know all too well what that could mean," Nick said looking at his hand.

"And we need to be in D.C. tomorrow," I said half as a question.

"I'll be ready," Nick nodded.

We flew to D.C. the following morning. I wasn't looking forward to my meeting with the police captain that hired me to find Boris. I had never failed to "get my man" until this case. I could tell that they weren't happy with my lack of progress and the huge expenses I had incurred. However, they still needed to apprehend him so they gave me thirty more days to find him. I left the meeting feeling a bit whipped, but I was determined not to disappoint them—or myself—again.

With one uncomfortable meeting out of the way, Nick and I headed to the other. How do we tell the authorities about aliens? Nick mentioned that his father had an old military buddy who still worked for the Pentagon. He had his dad set up an appointment for this afternoon.

We stopped for lunch and then headed to the Pentagon. We were stopped at the gate. We told the guard that we had an appointment with General Billings. Fortunately, the guard had our names on his list. We showed our ID and were escorted in.

"Get in the jeep," the guard said, "and The M.P. will drive you to the general's office."

General Billings met Nick with a strong handshake and a hearty clap on the back.

"General, this is Joe, my business partner." Nick pointed in my direction and the general shook my hand. I was sure my hand wouldn't be of any use after that handshake, but I took it like a man.

"Good to see you again, Nick. It's been a few years. Now what can I do for you boys?" General Billings gestured us to take a seat.

"I'm not really sure how to say this without sounding crazy, so I will just cut to the chase," Nick said holding up his finger. We can only share this with someone who will take us seriously, and it has to be someone we can completely trust. General, my dad says he can trust you, and has, with his life."

"This sounds rather serious," General Billings responded, not taking his eyes off of Nick's hand. "Tell me, Nick, what's so urgent that you two flew all the way to Washington D.C. to talk to me?"

Nick hesitated, too long I guess, because General Billings seemed to get impatient.

I jumped in and began my story with the hunt for Boris. I told him about the necklaces that could see the Morph people, about the mother ship and smaller spaceships. The general looked up with raised eyebrows when I used the term Morph. I explained how I came up with that name. I left out the part about where we had gotten the necklaces, hoping with all of the alien talk he wouldn't think to ask.

I continued my story up to the part about the farm and the renters who had disappeared.

"And before you put us into straight jackets, General," Nick piped up, "you have Morphs working in the Pentagon."

The General didn't say a word; he simply reached for the phone and talked quietly, almost in code. Nick and I stared at each other with worried looks on our faces. The General hung up the phone and told us, commanded us, to follow him.

We went down a long corridor to an elevator that took us up two floors. We then climbed a small flight of stairs and ended up on the roof of the Pentagon, standing to the side of a helicopter pad. Two guards climbed out and motioned for us to get in.

CHAPTER TWENTY-THREE

The pilot handed us headsets and then took off.

General Billings did not come with us. This was a bit disconcerting because he was our only connection to the outside.

"Where are we going?" Nick asked the pilot. There was no answer. Five minutes later, we were over the ocean. I felt a bit uneasy because it wasn't like there were any islands close to shore where we would land. *Where were they taking us?*

Just as I was about to tell Nick that I thought this was all a big mistake, a submarine came right up out of the ocean. It was such an incredible sight that we forgot all about our situation. Water poured off the deck as the submarine floated to the surface. Two sailors came up onto the deck and guided the helicopter down.

We stepped inside the submarine and were greeted by a civilian who introduced himself only as Marcus.

"Follow me, gentleman," he said just a bit curtly.

We were taken to a small room where we were asked to tell our story. We briefed Marcus on everything we knew about the Morphs.

He ordered us to keep all knowledge of these alien creatures quiet and had us sign official papers stating this was a government-sanctioned order.

Marcus then took us to a big room at the bottom of the submarine. On that floor was a small body of water, out of which came a very small submarine. We were ordered into the sub, but I wasn't very eager to go from cramped quarters to really cramped quarters. The guards just stood there glaring, so Nick and I climbed in, followed by Marcus.

Marcus took the front seat and we sat just behind him. It was not long before we were at an underground city. Nick muttered something about it being a "mind-blowing experience." I nodded my head in agreement, but he wasn't looking at me. The city was absolutely majestic.

It was made up of six large, clear, dome-shaped structures. There was a circle of small submarines patrolling the area around the city. The submarine we were on went under the city and then came up under a dome called the Jupiter. We all got out of the mini-sub and stepped up into the dome. The platform that we stepped out onto looked like the opening to our cave back home. Instead of being made of rock, though, this one was metal.

A woman in civilian dress met us on the platform. "It's good to meet you two," she said extending her hand. She introduced herself Sarah Hardy.

Sarah showed us around Jupiter. The main dome room was filled with computers. Funny, I thought. Every one working was a civilian. The only people in uniform were the military police.

Sarah told us she had an important meeting to attend, so she would meet up with us tomorrow to continue the tour.

"Please escort Nick and Joe to their rooms," Sarah instructed the M.P. who had suddenly appeared. With a nod goodbye to us, she quickly left the room.

We followed him down a long hallway to our room. He unlocked the door for us and admonished us to stay put. We were told that we could only leave the room to use the bathroom and shower. "Guests are not allowed access to any part of the city without official escort," he said. A guard would be posted outside our room at all times. It sounded like a warning.

We stepped inside the room and saw that we would be sleeping in a bunk bed.

"Nick you can have the bottom bunk because of your hand. I can handle the top. I'm only missing a molar," I grinned.

"Thanks, Joe, Nick grinned back. "Need help chewing your next steak? I'll gladly return the favor!"

We had a good laugh and settled in for the night. I pulled back the curtain and looked out at the water. It was so clear we could see the brilliant colors of the fish as the light played across them. The reflection of the domes cast some shadows across parts of the water, and the glowing of a sea snake showed up brightly in those dark shadows. It was eerie and beautiful at the same time. Just like the rest of this underground city.

The next morning, two marine guards informed us that it was 0600 hours. I couldn't believe how well we slept; it must have been the quietness of the place. We only had time for a quick shower and shave. Although I didn't much like being ordered around, I didn't want to make waves.

Then realizing what I had just said, I shook my head—making waves. I was definitely too hungry to laugh at my own jokes.

We were escorted to the mess hall for breakfast. I hoped that submarine food was really as good as everyone said. *Maybe it was even better in underground cities.*

It *was* as good as they said. Nick and I were served scrambled eggs, hash browns, sausage links, biscuits, and lots of country gravy to pour over those biscuits. The sea air must have perked up our appetites because Nick and I didn't have any trouble eating everything set before us. Just as we finished, Sarah joined us. She apologized for leaving us so abruptly last evening, but said the wait was worth it as we were going to be shown something most spectacular.

'What?" Nick asked, shoving the last bite of biscuits and gravy into his mouth.

"I don't want to spoil the surprise," Sarah smiled secretively.

We chatted casually over a few cups of coffee before she stood up. She led the way to another dome named Sagittarius. We navigated through some long underground tunnels and through rooms that looked like storage rooms before we stopped at large double doors. The guard unlocked both sides and we stepped aside as he pulled them open. To our amazement, we were looking at a real space ship. It was a smaller version of the mother ship. Sarah explained that the space ship had crashed into the ocean two years ago, and that it took two months to retrieve it. The ship was then sent here so we could study it.

"All but one of the Morphs—I understand that is your term for the aliens—on board the ship were dead. We discovered that when they were killed, their bodies turned to ash. But when they died of natural causes, their bodies remained intact."

"We also know they can communicate with each other telepathically, but only at short distances— maybe a mile at the most. They like warmth, but like us, they can survive in the cold for a while."

Suddenly, a set of stairs quietly descended from the center of the spaceship. Sarah motioned us to climb up into its belly. It was surprisingly roomy inside. We had entered into the control room. Sarah said that it was too damaged to fly, but if it could, the navigation would be done from this room.

Nick asked Sarah what kind of fuel it used.

"We will discuss that later," Sarah said a bit secretively. "There is still a lot we are learning about this spacecraft. It is being reverse engineered as we speak. Be sure we will figure it out."

She also told us that the Morphs had been here before. Older maps had been discovered on board the ship, which led us to believe they had been coming for centuries. She added that even with the amazing speed of this ship, it would still take about two weeks to get to earth.

We continued watching as dozens of men worked on the spaceship. They were dissecting it one small section at a time. We tried to stay out of the way, but it was fascinating to watch them work with such painstaking care. Even the smallest thing could be a major clue.

Nick asked Sarah where the Morph bodies had been taken. Sarah answered that most were cryogenically frozen. "Some are being dissected so that we can get a better knowledge of their genetic makeup."

She then asked us once again to follow her. I hated to leave the control room, but there was more to see. Sarah then led us to the library where thousands of books were neatly arranged on rotating shelves.

"They sure read a lot of books," Joe commented.

I picked one up. It was written in a language I had never seen before. I watched a table full of people taking notes; they were trying to learn the language. One man told me that it had taken him months to decode their alphabet, while another said he could now understand much of their language, but it was a very slow process.

Sarah said the reason Nick and I were here was so we could share what we knew of the Morph people. We were going to have a meeting after lunch where we could tell more of our story. Most of what we knew was how violent they were, I thought.

Lunch was brought into the library. We sat away from the books and relaxed for a bit. There were about twelve of us sitting around the table. "It's open mike," Sarah told us. "Anyone who had information to share should feel free to speak up. The quicker we learn about these people, the safer we will all be.

"Joe," Sarah asked looking in my direction, "would you start by telling your experiences and observation regarding these creatures? Start from your very first encounter with them. Remember that no detail is too small to share."

"Ok," I said, standing up. It was easier to think if I could pace a bit as I talked. I spent the next hour sharing what I knew.

"How were you able to see the Morphs, Joe?" Sarah asked.

"I was given a necklace by a friend. Wearing that necklace allows me to see them as the monsters they are. To the naked eye, they look just as human as everyone in this room."

Nick spoke up next. He told of his encounters and held up his hand as proof of his horrible experience with them.

A man who introduced himself as Alex said that as he slowly deciphered the books, he realized that these aliens had been coming to earth for thousands of years. At first, they came every hundred years or so. Mostly they came for the minerals to fuel their ships as they flew to other planets.

Another gentleman by the name of Ralph noted that humans were not on earth when these aliens first began coming to our planet.

"I can only imagine their surprise when they first saw us. That's why there are so many recorded sightings. They have been coming for a long, long time and some in this room think the dinosaurs may have been their first victims."

Sarah spoke up and shared that the government was working on a virus to kill these Morphs.

"So far, they have been immune to anything that we have thrown at them. We are years away from finding anything that works."

Suzanne spoke next. "We now know the spaceships frequent earth all the time. Although it takes weeks to get here, there are always dozens on the way."

Cheryl stood up to say that the Morph people take us for pets on their planet. "Once a human enters the spaceship, they become six inches tall. They love us and care for us just like we do our pets here. Selling pets is a big business there."

Julian was the next to add what he knew.

"There are groups of Morphs who think the pets are a nuisance. They are very powerful. They think of us more as rats rather than pets and would like to exterminate us. Not just on their planet, but on our own."

Borden spoke up saying, "We think they have tried several times already. Throughout the years there have been diseases that have wiped out thousands upon thousands of people. We think they might have been responsible for the bubonic plague, small pox, cholera, and many other influenzas."

Marcus came into the room saying, "Joe, I have a message for you. Word just came that Boris was seen in Appleton, Missouri."

"What?" I exclaimed. "I would have bet anything that Boris had been captured by the Morphs. He had disappeared so completely. I guess my visit here is over."

Sarah spoke up. "I'll make arrangements for you to get back, Joe." Then they left the Sagittarius dome.

They walked back to the submarine and were ready to board when Sarah hesitated.

"Nick, would you mind staying on?" Sarah asked. "Just for a bit? I could use your help."

" Are you okay with that, Joe?" Nick asked.

"No problem, Sport. I'm going to be busy looking for Boris, anyway," I said giving Nick a knowing look.

Nick turned back to Sarah. "Sure, but all this scientific stuff is way out of my league."

CHAPTER TWENTY-FOUR

The next day, I arrived in Appleton, Missouri. After getting my hotel, the first thing I did was to go to the homeless shelter. They told me that Boris got a job at a local plastic factory making dishes. I got directions and decided to stake out the place before going in. I didn't want any surprises, nor did I want anyone to get hurt in the crossfire.

I didn't seem to have any luck because the shift had just ended. There were a lot of people in the parking lot, but I didn't see Boris. Then I saw a scruffy looking guy with a lunch pail. There he was! I made sure my .38 special was loaded and headed toward him.

He was standing alone, so I yelled out for him to freeze. Boris turned around to face me.

"You just don't give up do you, "Boris said not really asking a question.

"On the ground, now!" I shouted. But Boris just laughed and knocked the gun away from me. He grabbed me by the shirt and gave me a karate chop to the neck. I went down and he gave me a swift kick to the groin. While I was writhing in pain, trying to get up, he bent to the ground and picked up my gun. Laughing, he shot twice into my chest.

"I'm just too quick for you fools," Boris said grinning. He took off running with my gun still in his hand. I was glad that I was smart enough to have put on my bulletproof vest. My chest was bruised, but at least I was alive.

Once Boris left, witnesses came to my rescue. An elderly man helped me to my feet and suggested I get a safer line of work.

I felt like someone had taken a sledgehammer to my chest. Tomorrow I would come up with another plan—hopefully a better one. Boris was my toughest assignment so far.

Back at my hotel, I lay on my bed wondering if Boris had hoboed a train. I was mad that I had let him get the better of me. And I was especially mad that I let him take my gun. I had to figure out a way to let my anger become productive. I would sleep on it; some of my best ideas came in the night.

The next morning, I headed to the train station with some of the fliers I had made up weeks ago. Boris was a bit rougher looking, but still recognizable. I walked around for nearly an hour before one man said he looked like a guy who jumped the train heading for Wyoming. Another freight would be coming through in a bit and he was going to be on it. I was welcome to join him if I was serious about catching my man. We would have to wait out of sight until the inspectors made their rounds. I decided I might as well take this route. I have been on a plane, train, helicopter, bus, sub, and car looking for Boris. I may as well try the train. The hobo introduced himself to me simply as Ned and shook my hand.

Ned told me to do just what he did. When he said to jump I had better jump and jump fast.

He waited for the train to begin moving, slowly at first. He then hopped on. Ned held out his hand for me as the train began picking up speed. I felt a sting of pain when I stretched out my hand to grab his. I missed. I was still sore from those gunshots. I had to run faster now as the train was getting away from me. Ned held on with one hand and stretched his other hand out as far as he could. With a surge of determination, I made a run for it and grabbed Ned's outstretched hand. He yanked me in and I fell to the floor of the car. Fortunately for me, Ned was stronger than he looked. My guess is he had been doing this for most of his life.

We sat on some old folded cardboard boxes that looked like they had been used many times before. I saw an old coffee can with burnt toilet paper on the bottom and a small grate on top. Ned told me that was how most hobos make their coffee. They would swipe the toilet paper from gas station restrooms and dig through restaurant dumpsters for old coffee grounds.

"You can't part an old hobo and his coffee," Ned said emphatically. He then told me we should be in Casper by morning. I asked Ned what he used to do for a living. He said he used to be a physicist in Germany, but after an accident in his lab, he was banned from his profession. Two people were killed. Ned said his assistant pulled the wrong lever on an experiment, causing an explosion. The assistant was killed, as was an observer.

I was sympathetic and told him I was sorry to hear it. Ned nodded and continued with his story. "I came to the U.S. hoping to find a good job, but because of my accident, no one wanted to hire me in my field. So now, it's just odd jobs wherever I can find them. I move around a lot, trying to go wherever the sun is warmest. I hope one day my luck will change; but for now, I just keep going."

We were quiet for a bit, thinking about where we were going and what we needed to do. I knew I needed help with Boris. I wondered if Ned could be of help. He certainly was intelligent enough, and definitely strong, so I offered him a job working with me. Ned was excited about being a part of my search for Boris. He was a martial arts black belt, and thought it might come in handy. After nearly missing the train because of being shot, I thought so, too.

We finally arrived in Wyoming. I advanced Ned five hundred dollars. Surprised, but pleased, Ned thanked me. We stopped at the store to pick some clothes and supplies. Now we just needed a way to get around.

We rented a car and decided we would book rooms at the Wagon Wheel Hotel for a night or two. I looked at my room key; again, I was in Room 222. What are the odds, I thought. After getting settled in, I walked next door to get Ned for a late lunch.

Afterward, we began our hunt for the ever-elusive Boris. We were getting nowhere until someone suggested that we try some of the ranches on the outskirts of town. They hire day laborers and it was an easy place for someone to hide out.

We headed to Casper and enjoyed the wide-open spaces. The ranches were large and quite far apart. I knew we wouldn't have time to check all of the ranches, but we could get to a number of them.

Our first stop was at the Tumbleweed. We drove through the open gate and pulled off to the side to talk to a cowboy taking the saddle off his horse. He stepped over to our car to ask if he could help us. I showed him Boris' picture. He looked at it briefly and said that he hadn't seen this fellow, but he hadn't seen anyone for the last week. He had been out on the range mending fences. He pointed to the big house at the end of the driveway and said for us to go up there and check with them.

As soon as I pulled up to the house, a man in a black suit came out to greet us. I thought it was an odd choice of clothing for a man on a working ranch. He must have seen the curiosity on my face because he said that he had just gotten back from the morgue. He had to identify the body of his good friend who was shot and killed by an intruder.

I pulled out Boris' picture and showed it to the man. He grabbed the photo from my hand and threw it to the ground.

"That's him! That's the guy who killed my friend." The man went on to say that Boris stole his friend's truck and was caught in it early this morning. He was being held at the county jail.

I told him how sorry I was that the very man I had failed to apprehend had killed his friend. I then went on to explain how Boris had stolen my gun, and that I felt responsible for being a part of this man's death.

"Oh, no! Don't think that. This Boris man broke in and took whatever he could lay his hands on. When my friend tried to stop him, Boris grabbed a rifle and shot him."

I thanked him for his help and for the directions to the county jail where Boris was being held.

We headed to the jail and asked to see the sheriff. A few minutes later, he stepped out of his office and told me that I was out of luck.

"You can't see or talk to Boris," the sheriff informed me. "I have strict orders from the F.B.I. to keep him under lock and key until someone can get here to pick him up. I can allow you to identify him, to satisfy your need to know that he is for sure the one we have in custody."

I was allowed to look through the small window in the door that separated the main offices from the jail cells. There he was, sitting on the edge of the bed, pounding his fist into the pillow. I was satisfied that Boris was at the end of his run. I thanked the sheriff and we left. Our work here was done.

We decided to wait around until the F.B.I. took possession of Boris before leaving. We didn't have long to wait. The F.B.I. pulled up in a blue and white van, and before long they brought out a shackled Boris. It was a satisfying sight.

CHAPTER TWENTY-FIVE

Back at the hotel, Ned and I talked over beer and pizza. I asked him if he would like to get back into his old business.

He surprised my by saying, "No, I would love to open a bookstore. One where high school kids could come and hang out and get help with their studies. I would love to teach them science and have other tutors available to help them with their other classes."

"Where?" I asked simply.

"Los Angeles, I think. It's a very diverse city with so many opportunities for kids who need a helping hand. It really has nothing to do with money. It's hard being a kid today."

We laughed about how fast this job ended once I took him on board to help. "Boris must have gotten wind of your black belt status. It made him sloppy." I said.

He thanked me again for the advance. He pulled out the money and gave it back to me. He hadn't earned it, he said, and couldn't keep it. I didn't want to take it back, but didn't want to insult his integrity, either. I could tell he felt strongly about it, so I put the money back into my wallet.

We talked a bit longer about the bookstore and how he would set it up. I admired his selflessness, his desire to help those who just needed a chance. I told Ned that I had been left with a lot of money and had been instructed to put it to good use. Up to this point, only Nick had really followed through on that promise.

"You are a good man, Ned. It has been my profound pleasure to have run into you. I have to get back to Indiana, but I would like you to put some of my money to good use. Tomorrow, fly to Los Angeles and find a spot to open your bookstore. We will go to the bank first thing in the morning, and I will give you enough cash to get started. I'll have our accountant set up a bank account for your living expenses and for the renovation of whatever property you find. If you are half the man I think you are, you will be making it work in no time."

Ned was flabbergasted by my story and offer. He didn't know what to say except thank you over and over again. I was sure it would be money well spent.

THE CAVE JOURNALS

CHAPTER TWENTY-SIX

I finally arrived home. Steve met me at the door.

"Good to see you again, Steve. How long can you stay this time?" I asked.

"I'm home for a couple of weeks, and I want to enjoy every minute of it!" he responded, shaking my hand.

After a few minutes of casual conversation, we decided we would go for a swim before supper. Steve had ordered pizza and said there would be plenty for the two of us.

"Let's put some beers on ice," Steve suggested. Then we can really catch up. I hear you have been on a really tough case. Meet you at the bottom."

I could hear him yell all the way down the tube.

I was just a minute or so behind him and hit the water with a splash. The water was cool, refreshing, and just what I needed after a long flight.

We sat at our new tables and enjoyed catching up. Steve told me that he had finished his helicopter training and was now ready to put in some actual flight training hours.

He told me of some of his experiences, and I could tell that he was really happy fulfilling this lifelong dream of his.

"Okay, enough about me," Steve said. "Tell me about your latest case. And where is Nick? I thought he was with you?"

"It's a really long story," I laughed, "so be prepared for an all-nighter! Seriously, though, the pizza should be here any time. We won't hear the doorbell clear down here."

We went up the elevator, and by the time we got dressed, the pizza had arrived. We settled down at the kitchen table with our beer and food.

The first thing I did was tell Steve about the necklaces that Pam and Sherry had given each of us. I handed him his and told him that it really did work; it made the Morphs visible in their alien state. Steve put on the necklace and wondered if he would be afraid if he saw one. I hoped he would never have to find out. I filled him in on Gramps and the spaceships. It was more of a struggle to talk about

Maggie. I was missing her more and more everyday. Steve's look told me he could tell what I was feeling. I told him that all of this was happening while I was on my hunt for Boris. I covered half of the U.S. looking for him before he had finally been caught in Wyoming.

"And Nick?" Steve asked.

I was quiet for a moment. Nick's whereabouts are still top secret. "All I can tell you is that Nick is helping the government find a way to exterminate the Morphs before they kill or capture all of us."

Funny the whole time I was gone, I hadn't seen any morph people.

We decided it was early enough to take the Camaro out for a spin and maybe pick up some groceries while we were out. We cleaned up our mess and headed to Logansport. We drove around the countryside for a bit but all we could see was corn. We stopped at the grocery store, but Steve wanted us to sit in the car for a while to see if any Morphs showed up. We didn't have to wait long. Steve was shocked at the grisly looking aliens. I don't know what he expected. I don't think he knew either.

"We need Pam and Sherry," Steve said. "Is there any way to contact them?"

"Lets go to the graveyard and see if any of their equipment is left. If there is, they may be coming back." I suggested.

We found the crypt and went inside. The girls were just packing up the last of their equipment. Steve began telling them all about the Morphs in Logansport. "If only we could find a way to eliminate them," he said. The girls exchanged glances and reminded us that we had been given the necklaces for a reason. They knew all about the Morphs, as we called them, but couldn't interfere.

"For many years the Morphs were very active in Wyoming. They mined minerals until one day they dug up a triceratops graveyard. Thousands of these aliens died after being exposed to the bone dust. They stay out of Wyoming for the most part, now.

"We can't tell you what to do, nor can we do anything else for you. But we can tell you that if you could use the deadly triceratops bones in a virus, you might be able to rid your country of them once and for all." Pam said that maybe she had already said too much.

They were packing up the last of their supplies and needed to finish up. "It was good seeing you, Steve. Please say hello to Nick for us."

I said he was out of town on business, but Sherry smiled and said she knew exactly where he was!

We said our goodbyes and let them finish up their work. On our way out of the graveyard, two Morphs came up behind us. They had their weapons drawn.

"Don't move," one said. "You're both coming with us."

The next thing I knew, I was unable to move, except for my eyes. I could see Steve was frozen, too. We were like a couple of graveyard statues. I saw Pam and Sherry step out of the crypt and I could hear them talking about saving our butts—again. Their banter was a bit lighthearted, but I didn't see anything funny about our predicament. I don't know how long we were standing there, but we were suddenly able to move. There were two Morphs lying on the ground. Pam and Sherry had disappeared again. So much for not helping us!

The Morphs were still alive, but their weapons were gone. We didn't know what to do other then get out of there.

We headed home and grabbed a couple of beers and decided to get some sleep. The phone rang just as I was heading up the stairs. Washington DC was calling. The agent on the other end of the line had some disturbing news. Boris had escaped from the FBI van.

They were on their way to a federal prison when a small spaceship had hovered above the van. A red light beamed down and aimed directly at them. The entire van had disappeared. The two guards and the van had been found about ten miles down the road, but Boris was gone.

Zorko was unpleasantly intrigued by this human named Boris. He picked up his journal and began to read.

"I first began this journal praying that someone would find it and rescue me from a horrible fate. I am now writing this journal in hope that it will be found by someone with the same hatred I now feel for you pathetic human beings. My story has taken a turn for the good.

Once again, I was arrested by those who think I have done wrong. But you were wrong. I was merely looking out for myself.

I was on my way to a Federal prison somewhere on the east coast. They wouldn't even tell me where for fear that I, Boris, would once again rise up and free myself. They have not yet found a way to keep me locked up.

It was late at night when I was shackled to the bars in the back of the van. Four Federal agents were sent to escort me back to the pen. All of a sudden, the van began to shake and it was lifted high into the air. "Oh, no, not again," I cried, remembering my last abduction. But yes, I was beamed this time into the mother ship that hovered just above the trees.

A Morph grabbed me out of the van, and immediately it and the agents inside were dropped back to the ground, almost as if they were spit out. The Morph put me back into the book and tightened the straps saying, "Try to escape this time." I was placed on the bookshelf titled Criminals and was only talked to when it was mealtime. It was a long flight, and I was afraid.

We arrived on Sagitar and I was sent to Hitler's City, a small town on the outskirts. Before I was even off the truck, men claiming to be soldiers in Hitler's army grabbed me and looked me over. I had a choice, they said. I could be a soldier and fight for their cause or be given a menial job in the kitchen.

I was told that Hitler would soon be taking over the planet of Sagitar. Only those who fought alongside him would survive. I didn't like either choice, but I figured being one of Hitler's men would keep me on the right side of trouble.

My job is perfect. I recruit new men to Hitler's cause. I have become a respected soldier and have many loyal followers of my own. I pretend to follow Hitler and be loyal to him, all the while watching and learning. One day, I will rise up. One day I will be feared. One day I, Boris Petrov, outcast of Earth, will rule my own planet. I will rule Sagitar. I have two thousand years to plan. I pledge one day to come back to earth. And when I do, it will be to destroy those for judging me wrongly.

Zorko read with half interest Boris' lofty thoughts of himself. He would indeed get his due in Hitler City. But for now, he needed to learn more about Joe. He continued reading Joe's journal.

Not again. I thanked them and hung up. I wasn't in the mood to deal with Boris right now. I decided, instead, to call General Billings. I told him what I had learned about making a virus out of triceratops bones.

"Where did you get your information?" General Billings sounded a bit disbelieving.

"I spent some time researching Morph activity in Wyoming. I promised I would not reveal my source's name," I responded vaguely.

"You would have to make it into a solution and spray cities and towns almost like you were killing mosquitoes," I said, feeling almost sick at the thought. We kept our conversation brief and to the point. General Billings said he would pass the information to Sarah and the research team.

I slowly walked up the stairs, thinking about Boris, the Morphs, and Maggie. What happened to my simple life of go after the bad guy, catch him, and then start all over again? Now it's aliens, spaceships, and love.

Steve met me at the top of the stairs and said he overheard me talking about Boris.

"Maybe the Morphs inserted some kind of tracking device in him."

I agreed. We were dealing with an advanced

civilization.

CHAPTER TWENTY-SEVEN

A week later, Nick arrived home and was happy that Steve was back for a bit. After general catching up, Nick needed to bring Steve up-to-date on the current situation.

"Steve," Nick said, "I've been cleared to share with you what the military has found about the Morph civilization. It's amazing what research is being done in the underwater domes. The captured spaceship has given them great insight into these creatures. It was fascinating being part of Sarah's world, but I'm glad to be back home.

I then filled Nick and Steve in on the virus spray. "It's in the works, and soon there will be a prototype to use to see if it works as well as we want it to. The government has a list of communities that are heavily populated with Morphs. As soon as they are sure that there will be no adverse reaction by our own people, they will go ahead and try it out.

I had no sooner spoken these words, than the phone rang. It was Sarah informing me that they began testing the virus and it seemed to be working. "New York City, where we sprayed the virus, reported thousands of people missing. There is also a report of "people" leaving the city." Sarah said that they were probably Morphs headed to a spaceship to get help. And if that were the case, they would infect the others and most likely kill everyone on board the ship.

I thanked Sarah for the update and told her about the spaceships near where Maggie lived. I gave her the address in Vermont and she was going to check it out. I hoped she would find Maggie in the process. Before she hung up, Sarah suggested that I meet her in Vermont. Since I was familiar with the area, it would save them time. She also said that it seemed as though we had a large Morph population right here in our area, so she was having some virus delivered here.

Nick wanted to go, too, but I informed him that Sarah was having some of the virus delivered to our house and someone needed to be here to accept it. Because Nick could see the Morphs, he would have to help the military figure out where to distribute the spray. Steve would be gone soon, so Nick had to stay.

I flew to Vermont and was on my way to Maggie's ranch when I saw a flying saucer crash into a ridge close by. I rammed the gas pedal into the floorboard of my rental car. I hoped Sarah and her crew were not far behind me. I got as close as I could to the spaceship. Somehow, I needed to make sure it was safe to get out of my car. I stayed put for a few moments to make sure there was no movement. It seemed clear, so I stepped outside my car and moved closer to the spacecraft. It was on its side and the door was partly open. I stepped inside. There were bodies everywhere. This ship was just like the one in the dome, so I knew my way around. I searched every room, but I couldn't see Maggie or anyone else that looked familiar. In my haste to find Maggie, I had forgotten the effect being in the ship would have on me. I felt myself shrinking. That didn't happen in the spaceship in the dome, so I figured the ship must be pressurized. I quickly headed to the engine room.

Maybe if I pulled the pressure valve it would change the pressure in the spaceship. I was shrinking fast now, and could barely reach the valve. I didn't have the leverage to pull it, so I took a few steps back then ran full steam ahead, jumped up, grabbed the lever, and pulled it down.

It took a moment before I could tell if it was

working. Yes! I was inching my way back to normal size. I was surprised that the ship was still pressurized after such a crash.

I continued my search for Maggie, but she wasn't anywhere to be found. I entered the library where there were, naturally, rows and rows of books. Each row had a sign with pictures that showed what category of books it contained. Although I couldn't read the writing, the pictures I understood. One was of humans, and others of dogs, horses, plants, cars, trains—every type of earthly being and object.

I pulled a book from the human section and found a man deeply embedded in the middle of the front cover. There were straps around the book to hold it closed. I picked up another book and found the same thing. I went to the animal section and found a dachshund secured firmly in the cover. I took the book outside and unstrapped it. I was shocked to see the dog literally leap to the ground and begin barking. In no time it was full size. It almost looked like the dog on Maggie's farm.

I picked him up and he licked my face. I looked at the tag hoping for a name and phone number or some way to identify the owner. The dog's name was Schotzie. On the back was Maggie's name and phone number. I began to understand what was happening to the people who had been abducted

Suddenly Schotzie began to growl. I peered up the ridge where I saw three Morphs appear. Their weapons were drawn and aimed directly at me. I had no weapon, thanks to Boris, and nowhere to run. I stood very still. Even Schotzie quieted down. As the Morphs came within speaking distance, one said, "You humans think you have won. You are trying to annihilate my people, but you can't get us all. We will be back. And when we come, we will attack your people with a vengeance. We will show no mercy. The mother ship headed for home, and the rest of us are here until we can be transported back to our planet. We will fight till the end, starting with you."

"What brought you to Vermont," I asked, trying to show no fear in order to buy some time.

The Morph looked at me like I was stupid. "There are minerals here that we need in order to build and repair our ships. We have been very successful and have harvested enough mineral to build thousands of new ships."

I could barely hear it, but there it was. A helicopter appeared over the ridge. Men were hanging out the sides with their weapons aimed at the Morphs.

"Drop your weapons," a familiar voice rang loud and clear.

The aliens did as they were told. As soon as it was all clear, Steve and Nick jumped from the helicopter that had landed in the small clearing just beyond the spaceship.

Nick surveyed the scene and shook his head.

"Talk about good timing..."

"After you left home, General Billings called to say they had a report of a downed spaceship near Maggie's place. When we told him that you were on your way there, he became concerned for your safety. He sent a military plane for us and we flew in shortly after you arrived," He waved his hand toward the chopper filled with military men. "You see we came well armed!"

As the Morphs were being restrained, they began shrinking before our very eyes. They slipped their restraints and turned into birds not of this world. Within seconds, they had flown out of sight.

Suddenly, people and animals began stumbling out of the spaceship. Some were back to normal size because I had depressurized the ship. Others were still small and hadn't yet returned to normal. Military trucks, vans, ambulances, and fire trucks all converged on the scene. There were almost more authorities here than when I was trying to get Boris at the motel in Pennsylvania. It must be another slow day in the crime department.

We all watched as people and pets walked down the ramp from the space ship. Still no Boris or Maggie. There were hundreds of people being treated by medics. Some were severe enough to need hospitalized and were driven off in ambulances.

The last person to leave the space ship was Becky. She was so excited to see a familiar face that she gave me a big hug and thanked me for saving her.

Steve watched with more than casual interest as Becky and I talked. I wanted to hear more of her story.

It was nearly morning by the time the military gave an all clear, saying the spaceship was empty.

I could only surmise that Maggie was on the mother ship on her way to the Morph's home planet.

The only thing making me smile was the fact that Boris had been caught for good this time.

Bright lights in the sky caught our attention. When we looked up, we saw three smaller space crafts disappear in the night sky. It must have been the three Morphs that we had encountered earlier.

I thanked both Nick and Steve for being there for

me.

Nick nodded. "That's what friends do."

Steve could see how tired I was. He suggested that I get in the helicopter and let the military drive my car to the Army base.

I thought that was an excellent idea. As I climbed into the helicopter with Steve, Nick, and Becky, I saw a man pick up Schotzie and put her in a car and drive away. I thought that was a bit odd, but I was too tired to think, and my attention was more on the helicopter than the dog.

We were all in a bit of shock and rode in relative silence. Becky seemed the most anxious and needed to talk to someone about her experience. I suggested that she stay with us for a few days and tell her story to Sarah.

Nick thought that was a good idea and would call Sarah as soon as they got home.

CHAPTER TWENTY-EIGHT

The next day, a knock on the door woke me up. It was Sarah. Nick had called her to tell her about Becky, so she decided that she would come and deliver the virus spray in person.

The five of us had a quick breakfast and sat around the table while Becky shared with us the story of her abduction. She was a bit nervous having to relive her horrible experience, but once she started, she was able to tell us of her time on Sagitar with a detached voice.

"Once again I found myself strapped to a table on one of the transporter ships," she began. "There was a machine going back and forth over my head. As this machine moved from side to side, I had flashbacks of my life. I saw my Uncle Walt throwing corn feed on the ground and the chickens pecking at his feet. Then I saw my Aunt Zetta mending socks as she watched her husband in the barnyard. I also saw Grandma as she rocked me in that small Boston rocking chair of hers. Back and forth, back and forth.

"I saw myself on a bicycle with my brother Pete behind me on his bike. We were riding to the park just down the street from our house. We were playing kickball, and then my brother was getting beat up by three bullies. I also saw my family at a picnic, laughing and eating watermelon when a crop duster crashed into our picnic table. I saw my brother, my mom, and my dad—all dead.

"I saw myself at a funeral. A row of caskets all laid out in the church. I saw myself weeping at the cemetery.

"Becky needed to stop for a moment and compose herself. "I'm sorry," she said. "It seems like it happened just yesterday."

Steve put his arm around her and asked if she needed to stop for a bit.

"No," she said. "I need to do this.

"It was a strange thing, seeing all of these memories. I wasn't sure, at first, why they were doing this to me. Several times a day they hooked me up to this machine that moved around my head and kept the memories coming. I remembered being older and being at a police station. Then I was in a home for troubled girls. I saw myself running away, hitchhiking across the country.

If I turned my head, I could see a TV. Every memory that went through my mind, every event in my life showed up on that screen.

"I saw my boyfriend Zach pick me up when I was hitchhiking. I saw Zach shoot his way out of a bank. Then I saw him being mowed down by cops, so many cops.

"Years of memories came and went. I then saw myself sneaking into a man's hotel room, and him tackling me to the floor."

Becky shot a quick, embarrassed look at me.

"The monitor suddenly went blank, as that was the last memory I had," she continued. "Then a man picked me up in his hands, and put me on the cover of a book. The book and I were then placed in a box. I could tell I was being taken to another room. It turned out to be the library. The monster handling the box was tossing it around like a rag doll. Then I heard a man say, 'Careful, careful, we need them alive.' I heard the sound of machines moving the box I was in. Finally, everything was still.

"What seemed like only minutes later, I heard a

scraping sound that a box knife would make. I then saw light. The book I was in was lifted out of the box. A man gently held the book in his hands. He ran his fingers over me and patted the book cover, pleased with what he had. He then carefully placed me on a bookshelf.

"Every so often, someone would come by to feed me. They would stick a tube down my throat. A liquid that looked like pink medicine was fed to me. I could hear these monsters talking to each book as they fed them. They sounded so gentle.

"I didn't know what to think. Was I to spend the rest of my life trapped on the cover of a book? What was the purpose of having me here? What sinister plot was I part of?

"I was suffocating in this book. Please let me out was all I could think. I tried to move, but I was too tightly bound in the book. I just gave up. The only relief was sleep."

Sarah thanked Becky for sharing her story, as difficult as it was to dredge up the experience. Steve handed Becky a tissue and they stepped outside to get some fresh air and be alone.

Sarah said she had to get back so she said her goodbyes and headed back to the dome to share

Becky's information with the other team members.

CHAPTER TWENTY-NINE

Steve only had a few days of leave left and decided to drive Becky home. He would go straight back to the base from her house.

Nick and I spent the rest of the week coordinating with the mayors of the surrounding cities to have the virus sprayed. It had to happen simultaneously so that not one community would have time to escape. One drop of virus per one hundred gallons of water would be enough to kill the Morph population.

Three days later the spray got underway. Alleys, sidewalks, parks, even the exteriors of buildings were sprayed. Nothing was overlooked. By the time we had finished, these communities were so drenched that they looked as though a monsoon had come through.

A few days later, there was pandemonium

throughout the country. As the Morphs began to die out, their bodies disintegrated into ashes. Because the Morphs had immersed themselves so thoroughly into the business communities where they lived, their deaths caused major problems. Businesses from banks to grocery stores lost CEOs as well as tellers, clerks, and checkers. Employers and employees alike disappeared. Restaurants had no cooks. Waste companies had no garbage collectors. Even empty vehicles clogged the streets. As frustration mounted, looting and mugging increased. In the larger cities, riot after riot destroyed the downtown. Firefighters were gone. The police force was cut in half. Finally, a national emergency was called and the National Guard was sent in. But even they had lost men. It was weeks before order could be maintained. New politicians, business executives, employees, and public safety personnel were assigned to fill in the gaps.

True to the nature of Americans, though, once the chaos slowed, they began to rise to the occasion and work together to reestablish their communities. Trash was hauled away, businesses opened, vehicles were towed, and buildings were repaired. The country was coming together again. Our work was done.

My case was somewhat solved. I didn't exactly feel

as though I had really done my job. The Morphs took it out of my hands. It wasn't exactly easy to explain, but it was finally done. Nick and I took it easy for a while. I didn't take any new cases, but Nick remained active in his charity work. He and Sarah spent a lot of time together.

I spend every evening thinking of Maggie. I still wasn't sure if was in love with her, but I missed her just the same.

After a few months passed and we had caught up on things around the house, Nick said that we needed to go through all the supplies in the pockets.

It seemed like a daunting job because the many, many pockets were stuffed full of who knows what. We decided to do a quick inventory to see where our priorities should be. I inventoried the rations. There were cases upon cases of canned and dehydrated goods. I thought that much of this stuff should be donated to shelters all over the state. Nick went through emergency supplies, finding cases of flashlights, matches and the like.

He moved a crate of paper plates out of the way and discovered an old leather satchel. It had a moon and a sun etched on the front. On the back flap of the satchel was an etching of a book with a person next to it. Inside was a journal, a quill pen, and a dried out inkbottle. The journal appeared to have been written in the mid 1800s.

Excitedly, Nick called out for me to come look. We walked over to the table where he began reading the journal aloud.

To Whom it May Concern:

In the third pocket to the right of the entrance into this cave is a large rock that looks out of place. Behind it is a handle. Upon turning the handle, a door will open. Behind this door many adventures await.   Emil Edward Lipton, 1835

"What the...!" we both exclaimed at the same time. "Emil Lipton must be Howard's great-grandfather that he told us about."

"Jinx, you owe me a coke," Nick laughed.

"How about a beer instead," was my expected answer as I reached into the cooler. "I think I need more than one."

I sat back down at the table next to Nick and asked if he was up for another adventure. With the eagerness of youth, he grinned and said, "Why not?"

It was a lot to take in, so we called it a day. I took a swim and relaxed on our beach for a bit. When I went back upstairs, I heard Nick on the phone with Sarah. He told her about finding the satchel. They continued to talk for a while until Sarah said she had some information for me. Nick told Sarah that he loved her and sheepishly handed me the phone.

"Joe, remember that windshield looking object you found in Oregon? Well, we haven't figured out what it is made of, yet, but we know how it works. There's a very small lock on the side of the glass, so small it is difficult to see. If you switch it to unlock, you can stretch the glass in any shape you want. Then you lock it again. Once you release the lock, it returns to its original shape. And, Joe, the machine that makes the glass is in your area. It was sold to someone in Logansport. That's the reason there were was such a large Morph population there."

Before we hung up, Sarah gave me the location of that machine. I looked at Nick and asked, "Were you going to keep your romance a secret?"

Nick blushed, and said, "We seem to be hitting it off pretty well."

We decided to take a swim. We slid back down to the beach and as I stood up, I lost my balance and grabbed for the table to steady myself. I knocked it over and as it hit a rock, the glass popped out of the frame. I picked it up and noticed a tiny protrusion on the edge of the glass. I looked a little closer and it looked like the lock that Sarah had told me about. I unlocked it and the glass expanded. Nick helped me reform the glass, I locked it and we put it back in the table frame.

"Well, I'll be," I said, wondering how much of this stuff was in all of our homes.

I grabbed us another beer and we talked about what we needed to do next. "I think our new adventure will have to wait, Nick. We need to go see the guy who made this table."

The next day I remembered to take my backup .38. I removed it from the locked cabinet and put it in my holster on the inside of my jacket. We headed to the house where I bought the table. The furniture maker, Fred, was working in his garage with the door open. We walked around his yard pretending to look at the furniture that was for sale.

He came up to us, and when he saw me, he asked how the furniture was working out. I told him that I had knocked over the table, but the glass didn't break or even crack. I wondered what kind of glass would be that strong. He hemmed and hawed a bit and looked somewhat flustered. After questioning him a bit more, he admitted that he had helped himself to the glass from the abandoned factory down the street. He said the factory had been deserted for years, so who would know or even care.

"No one was using the stuff, so I figured it was left behind when the factory closed."

"Fred, can you take us to the factory?" I asked.

"Sure thing," he said a bit relieved that we weren't interested in making a big deal out of his pilfering. As we drove to the factory, Fred told us the building was almost a landmark. It was originally built in 1720.

"As time went by," Fred continued, "the owners became very secretive. People began to wonder if the government was using it for something classified."

"From some of the stories I'd heard and old pictures I'd seen, there used to be a fort surrounding it. There were armed men in towers watching...but no one really knew what they were watching out for."

"Eventually, the town grew, people got busy, and the rumors died down. Everyone lost interest in it."

"Then sometime in the late 1800s, the fort burned down leaving only the glass factory standing. It eventually shut down and became just another old abandoned building. Surprisingly, in the early part of the 1900s, the glass factory was rebuilt and it reopened. We never knew who the new owners were, but it didn't stay open long, maybe another twenty years or so. I've been helping myself to the glass for years and no one has ever had an issue with that or with my tables until today."

We arrived at the deserted factory and were able to go right in. We saw the manufacturing area and the large machine used to form the glass. The machinery fascinated Nick, but I wanted to know what materials were used to make the glass. I hunted for an office of some kind. I found a rather large room with several desks and built-in cabinets. I opened one drawer after another looking for anything that might have some answers.

The desks had nothing in them except old office supplies. I tried the wall cabinets. One of them had old file drawers. As I rifled through the yellowed papers, I found what looked like a supply list. I took it back to Nick and showed it to him and Fred. They were sure that it was a list of items used to manufacture something. The problem was that we had never heard of some of the ingredients listed on it.

Nick suggested we show it to Sarah. Her team may

have isolated some of the items used to manufacture the glass. We took all of the glass that was left and headed back to Fred's house, grateful we were in his pickup.

I wanted to get this list to Sarah right away, so we stopped at the Post Office. Nick just happened to have Sarah's address.

CHAPTER THIRTY

Nick and I got up early the next morning. The Morphs were gone, Boris was captured, and the glass situation was in very capable hands. We were ready for another adventure. We headed down to the cave. We packed all of the flashlights we could carry and headed for the third pocket on the right. We looked closely at the rocks. Only one was just a shade lighter than the others. It wasn't obvious unless you were looking for something different. I gave it a push and it easily rolled away. Sure enough, we saw a long, brass lever imbedded in the rock wall that had been hidden behind the rock.

Nick reached in for his knife, pried the lever away from the wall, and pulled it back. Immediately, a rock door opened up. I shined my flashlight in and saw torches lining both sides of a passageway.

I took a matchbook from my backpack and lit a torch. We lit one torch after the other as we carefully walked the passageway. We had walked a good mile or so before we came to a room. We stepped inside but saw nothing except a bed and an old blanket. We continued on down the passage and came to a second room that was furnished just as sparsely as the first. We did find, though, a knife sticking out from under the old metal bed. Nick examined the rusty knife. The handle had had some strange letters engraved on it. He took the bandana from around his neck and wrapped the knife in it. He stuck it in his backpack to examine later.

We left that room and continued on. The passage widened into a room that was at least a city block wide. What we saw astonished us both. It was a graveyard full of dinosaur bones. Some were twenty feet high. I recognized the obvious and every kid's favorite, the T-Rex. Nick recognized the Spinosaurus and the Velociraptor. There were many others we didn't know.

We walked through the sea of dinosaur bones, trying not to disturb them. We stepped around fossilized teeth bigger than either of us. Nick climbed on top of one and sat on it like he was riding a horse.

As we walked through the never-ending bone yard, we wondered how they all got here in this cave. The room began to narrow by half. We could smell dampness as we walked farther on and soon saw a small river just ahead.

I took off my shoes and socks and began to wade across to the other side. Nick saw a bridge up ahead, so I put my shoes back on even though the cool water felt good on my tired feet. We crossed the bridge where the room continued to narrow. It almost felt as though the room was slowly closing in on us. We had come to the end of the cave.

"What now?" Nick asked.

I pointed my flashlight along the back wall of the cave. There was a small opening just big enough to crawl through. I went first and Nick followed. Luckily for us, there were more torches. Our flashlights were no match for the large torches lining the walls of this even bigger room. It was amazing. There were several smaller rooms shooting off from this one large room. Nick said they appeared to be carved out rooms rather than natural rooms.

We wanted to search each small room, but were ready for a break and food. We pulled out our sandwiches and canteens and sat on the surprisingly dry floor.

We got our energy back and decided that it was too

much for us to be able to search them all, but we did want to work for a while longer. We didn't find much. Nick found an old gun that looked like the ones used by the Morphs. I had seen this gun way too many times. I pulled the trigger but nothing happened. I was sure it was too old and probably needed a good cleaning.

As we moved from room to room, we noticed they varied in size. "This large one must have been reserved for the Morph officers," Nick said.

"I'm sure it was," I said looking at some star maps I had found.

As we looked around the big room, I saw another room; it was another library. I'd been in more libraries these past few months than I'd ever been in in my entire life!

I pulled out one of the books from off the shelf. There was a dinosaur on the front of the book. It wasn't a picture of a dinosaur or a drawing of a dinosaur, but a real fossilized dinosaur.

"Nick," I called. "Look at this."

"A T-Rex," Nick said. "Too bad it's dead. I'm surprised the Morphs left this behind. They must have been in a big hurry." He pulled more books from the shelf. "Interesting," he continued. "They all have prehistoric creatures on the covers."

We could only look at the pictures because the book itself was written in a different language. We didn't know what the books were about, but the photos of the dinosaurs were fascinating.

"I wonder what really happened to the dinosaurs and the Morphs," Nick said thoughtfully.

"It could have been that big meteor that hit the earth," he continued. "Maybe it wiped out these big boys. It's confusing because the photos look so modern.

"I wonder if, after the Morphs left the first time, the dinosaurs came here to die. You know, kind of like elephants do? Then when the Morphs came back and began modernizing everything, they came across the triceratops. It must have made them sick and they had to leave before they were all killed off."

We stood between rows of bookshelves, amazed at the volumes before us. We pulled book after book off the shelves to see the fossils of extinct animals on the covers. We had several dozen books in a stack when we heard a whirring sound as if a machine had suddenly started up. The shelves began to move slowly. The bookcase was coming straight toward us. By the time we realized there was another bookcase behind us, it was too late. We were about to be crushed. There was nowhere to go except up and that wasn't possible. Just before we became extinct, the bookcase stopped. We had some difficulty squeezing between them, but Nick managed to get out first. *Note to self: start working out again!*

"Well, would you look at that," Nick exclaimed in wonder.

I looked to my right and saw a tunnel. I looked to my left and the tunnel continued on. The entire area was lit up and not with torches. It was a lighting system way beyond anything we had ever seen. And running the whole length of the tunnels were train tracks. Right in front of us was a handcar sitting on the tracks. Like a kid at a carnival, Nick ran up to it and climbed on.

"Let's take it out for a spin," he grinned.

"I'm game," I replied. Let's go!"

We took the right tunnel, seesawing back and forth. "I wonder if this is the adventure Lipton was thinking about?" Nick laughed.

We got going pretty good when Nick pulled the brake lever. We jerked to a stop. "I just wanted to make sure they worked," he said.

"Next time, give me a heads up," I said, barely holding on. Nick just grinned.

We had gone several miles and our arms were getting pretty sore. We came upon another station. We stopped and went in. The station was full of small dressing rooms full of every kind of military uniform you could ever need: Air Force, Army, Navy, and Marine. Some with stripes, others with medals.

Nick was busy rummaging through the uniforms and turned to ask me a question, but I was not there. He yelled out to me in a bit of a panic. When I stepped out of the dressing room in a general's uniform, Nick fell to his knees laughing. I thought I looked rather dashing.

I changed back into my clothes and we got back in the handcar and went about another mile down the tracks until we came to another station.

This one was a mess hall. There were trays full of dishes, cups, and silverware. In the back, there were huge pots and pans, stoves, grills, and a very large-capacity dishwasher.

Nick's stomach began to growl after walking around the kitchen. We took out our rations and ate in the dining room.

Nick had packed white chicken with rice and I had

beef stroganoff. They were cold and tasteless, but our stomachs were satisfied. We washed it down with water from our canteens. As usual, we got sleepy after our meal. It was late, so Nick suggested we rest for a few hours. There was no telling what tomorrow would bring.

I agreed and volunteered to stand guard for a couple of hours while Nick slept. Then Nick would watch while I rested. It seemed a strange thing to need a lookout, but after the things we had experienced recently, it made perfect sense. Nick asked what I was going to do for two hours. I pulled out my Sam Spade book.

Nick smiled and closed his eyes. I got so caught up in my book that I forgot to wake Nick after two hours.

I let him sleep a bit longer before giving him a shake. "Thanks for the extra sleep," Nick said, grabbing the Sam Spade book from me.

"No problem," I said. "Happy reading."

Nick didn't usually read detective books. He was more into mafia type books. But he found the book so gripping, he let me sleep until he finished the book. We had no reason to hurry.

We hopped back on the handcar and rode for another few miles. We came to our fourth station. I knew immediately what the train station was for. Recruits. I could tell by the yellow footprints on the floor. I remembered my cousin Jack telling me that when he first went into the Army, all the recruits would stand on yellow footprints waiting to get their barracks assignments.

Once inside the station, the yellow footprints split into three separate directions, each leading to a different desk. We looked into the drawers and found files on each of the new recruits. The Morphs were giving their people new identities and jobs. They were well organized.

We headed out again only to find we were at the end of the tracks and an eight-foot stone wall loomed before us. We went back inside to see if there was a new tunnel hidden there. We tapped walls, floors, moved furniture and even stood on desks to check for false ceilings. There were no leads inside.

This must be the end of the line this direction, so we decided to head back to the first station where the library was.

As Nick pulled the reverse direction lever, he saw a seven-foot grate on the wall next to the tracks. The grate blended in so well, you had to be right next to it to see it.

Nick yelled that he wanted to see what was beyond the grate.

"Of course," I muttered. My stomach was beginning to growl big time.

"Well, I'll be," I said aloud. "We walked past that grate at least a half a dozen times."

We pried open the grate and found that we were staring at another set of train tracks. There was another handcar just a few feet ahead. We stepped onto the handcar and started seesawing back and forth and back and forth. I wasn't sure how long my arms were going to last. Nick didn't seem to be having quite the trouble I was. He must have been doing a lot of swimming while I was gone.

We moved slowly and looked around more carefully. We saw signs that seemed to give the Morphs instructions on how to act in public: *Know Your Neighbor, Don't Linger in Large Crowds, Keep in Constant Communication With Your Contact Person*. There were reminders everywhere.

After about three miles farther into the cave, we discovered an underwater lake. To our amazement, there was a submarine. It was moored by a rope tied to a large rock. We assumed we had permission to come aboard and didn't hesitate.

I had seen subs like these before. They only submerged a few feet. They were more for entertainment purposes. I had seen them at waterfront carnivals. It had one long lever in the front of the sub for moving backwards and forwards. There was a smaller lever that moved the fin in the back.

Now that we had it figured out, it was too tempting to not take it out for a spin. It could seat ten people, which meant that ten morphs at a time entered the cave.

Nick climbed in while I untied the sub. I closed the hatch as I climbed in. Nick crossed his fingers that it would start up. He pushed the starter and lights suddenly lit up the instrument panel. "We're good to go, Skipper," Nick chortled. "We should have kept some of those uniforms we found yesterday."

As the lake got deeper, Nick hollered back for me to let in water. I turned the valve and could feel the submarine begin to sink. I pushed forward. I could hear Nick yell, "Dive, dive!" I turned the valve wide open. We were headed straight into a wall. The submarine sank fast, barely missing the wall.

"That was too close," Nick said. And told me to let

out some of the water. He wanted to stay as close to the ceiling wall as possible. We saw light from above, so we knew we could now surface in the part of the lake that was open.

We docked alongside nine other subs. They were all painted to look like dragons. As we climbed out, we saw a large house on a hill above the dock. We tied off and walked part way up the hill. Nick said he knew where we were. We were behind a carnival that was open year round. We continued up the hill toward the house where there were *Private Property* signs posted all over.

Of course we ignored them and knocked on the door anyway. There was no response. We were sure the house was empty, so we tried the door and it was unlocked.

Nick decided to go into the house. It was more like a hotel, as there were ten bedrooms. And there were books everywhere. After being in so many Morph libraries, it was nice to see books written in English. There were books on politics, religion, and business. There were cookbooks, math books, English books—nearly every subject imaginable was represented by at least one book.

After looking around for a bit, I didn't find anything else of interest in the house. On our way out, Nick accidentally kicked over a trashcan. When he set it upright again, a false door opened behind it. The door was small, barely enough room to squeeze through. He told me to follow him in, and watch the door to make sure it didn't close behind us. The room was filled with star maps, most of which were in English. One map was of the Morph home planet called Sagitar. The topography of Sagitar resembled earth. It had oceans, mountains, and plains. It looked enough like earth that I figured humans could live there with relatively little trouble.

We also discovered an arsenal of weapons. Mostly, it seemed, Morphs liked ray guns. There were a couple of rifles that looked like one of those big water guns that kids play with. I also found stacks of bills containing ten thousand dollars each. This must have been escape money because there was a list of addresses all over the country where Morphs would be safe if they were in any sort of trouble. We finished inspecting the house but needed to get back to the sub. It would be dark soon, and we hadn't eaten all day.

We wanted to get back to the tracks to see what was on the other side of the library. The return trip in the submarine was quicker. I got the hang of the maneuvering in no time.

I dreaded getting back on the handcars. My arms

and back were sore from miles of continual pumping. But, we didn't have any other choice, so we got back on and passed the library to the next station.

I could tell as soon as we pulled up, that this station would be Nick's favorite. He was all smiles. Printing presses, ID cards, blank drivers' licenses, and birth certificates were everywhere. Even library cards, ironically, sat in neat stacks on the table. Everything a Morph would need for identification was made right here. Nick wasn't the only one dealing in false identification papers!

The Morphs were extremely organized. They had files of every Morph that had come to earth. Files with thousands of pictures, before and after landing on earth, were cataloged along with current names and addresses. This was a great find. It would be immensely helpful in tracking down whatever Morph people were left on earth. I stuffed a few files in my pack so that I could show Sarah exactly what we had found.

We had to keep moving. We stopped at the next train station that was like every woman's dream shopping mall. Rooms were filled with high-end jewelry, watches, purses, ties, shoes, clothes, and fashions. Everything that was needed to make a Morph blend into society was in this one station.

One-stop shopping was never easier!

I wondered why one station was full of military clothing and paraphernalia while the other one was nothing but civilian clothing and accessories.

"Probably because they want Morphs in all areas of human society," Nick responded. "Some will join the military while others will become businessmen, teachers, and the like. My guess is, though, that having a high Morph population in the military is part of their plan."

"Makes sense to me," I said.

We got back on the handcar and continued on to the end of the tracks. Only a wall loomed before us. We looked, but again, there didn't appear to be a door. We checked every inch of the wall, trying to find some type of opening, or lever, or knob, or something. Nick even looked closely at the walls, going up and down the track. I walked across the track and shone my flashlight over the walls. I noticed a couple of pockets in one wall and called Nick over to see. I moved my flashlight around, and suddenly the room lit up revealing a panel with symbols. I pressed on the symbols, but nothing happened.

Nick told me he seen those symbols somewhere, but

he couldn't remember just where. They must correlate somehow with the symbols on this panel.

We looked around but saw no sign of them anywhere. We went through all the desk drawers. We checked out a couple of the other rooms, but didn't see the symbols anywhere.

"Nick we have been at this for two days. Let's just go home and think this through over a cold beer and an extra large pizza." I pointed to the handcar and said, "Let's go."

Before long, we were in our personal cave headed toward the elevator.

The first thing we did was eat some real food. No pizza. Nick barbecued hamburgers while I made homemade fries. Snacking on chips and dip didn't spoil my appetite one bit. We sat at the table, barely awake, struggling to make sense of the events of the last two days. We couldn't, so we just crashed.

CHAPTER THIRTY-ONE

The next morning, I found Nick cleaning up from the night before. I sat at the table drinking my coffee. I wasn't awake yet; I almost felt numb. The events of the past two months were taking its toll on all of us, and I longed for my old life back.

Nick sat down at the table. "We must have missed something." He turned his coffee cup round and round in his hands. I could see his finger was healing up nicely, but I still felt bad for what he had gone through.

"Maybe we need to start again at that first station. I know we saw those symbols somewhere. Why don't we go back down to the cave and pull that lever again, and start all over?"

That's when it hit me. "Nick, I have it! I know the

answer to the code. When Lipton wrote that journal, he was talking about the adventure being behind the pocket door with the code. He wasn't talking about the train station or the submarine. Those places weren't around when he was alive. Remember the satchel had symbols on the front and the back."

We both rushed to the elevator to the cave. We got the satchel and headed back to the pocket with the symbols. Once there, I told Nick to press the moon button and then to press the sun button. We heard a clicking sound. I then had Nick press the book symbol, and lastly press the tiny person. The cave began to shake and small pebbles fell on us. Just then, a large room opened before us.

Standing in the center of the room was a big spaceship several stories high. It wasn't as big as the mother ship, but was much larger than the other spacecraft we had seen.

"Unbelievable," Nick said, standing directly underneath it. The ship was completely black. It was encircled with blue and red lights just like he had seen in the movies and in person.

It was saucer shaped and Nick found a ramp leading up into its belly. I followed him up the ramp.

It wasn't like the other ships I had been in. Once

inside I could tell it was made of glass that had been tinted black. We could see through the glass to the outside, but the tint prevented us from seeing inside the ship. Here was the reason the factory was making that special glass in Logansport. The morph people were building a mother ship here on earth. There were control panels in the middle of the room, and a windshield covered the entire middle section.

We continued exploring and found a room with ten operating tables. Each table had a small machine above it. The machines were on hinges so they could be pulled down over someone's head. We both figured that was how the Morphs read Becky's mind. Joe saw a printer next to the bed. It had printed out some strange words that neither of us understood.

We then walked through a room with printing presses. There were hundreds of books. Nick found a machine that appeared to make impressions of human shapes. All the books had leather straps around them.

Nick then went back into the hallway and found rows of completely furnished bedrooms. The rooms were like small apartments.

We moved on to the end of the hallway where there was a down staircase. We were now on another level of the ship. We passed a mess hall, a library, and what looked like a recreation room.

We went down one more flight of stairs and passed a hospital. We then came across a park that had strange looking toys. This must be where the Morph kids practiced using their muscles and changing their form. There were obstacle courses requiring them to change shape several times before reaching the end.

One of the courses was a long, narrow tube. In order to go through this one, the Morph child would have to become snakelike in shape. Another one was way above our heads. They would have had to change into a small bird to get through the hoop. This must be how those three Morphs near Maggie's ranch learned to turn into birds.

We continue on down yet another flight of stairs and arrived at a science lab. There were hundreds of test tubes filled with colored liquids and body parts. We wondered if they were the same parts taken from the bodies of Orval Beck's crew. The sight sickened us.

The strangest room we found was full of little robots. They were of different shapes and sizes. I figured they were probably made to resemble animals on Sagitar.

Nick tried to figure out how to turn one on. The robot looked like a mix between a rabbit and a squirrel. He hit a switch and laser beams shot out of the robot animal's eyes. I dove for cover as the beam shot right past my head. The desk I was standing next to disappeared into a puff of smoke. The robot was on the move now shooting laser beams at anything in sight. Other robots disintegrated as the robot moved around the room.

Nick was franticly trying to shut the robot down, while at the same time, trying to stay out of the way of the laser beams; but the little robot was too fast. Its head spun in circles as it found more objects to disintegrate.

I found a blanket and threw it over the moving robot. Nick was finally able to shut it down.

It was time to stop playing with dangerous toys, so we moved on through the spaceship to a room that looked like it belonged to a commanding officer. There was an oversized desk with flight plans drawn on a map. It looked like it had all the places marked where the Morphs mined minerals. I wondered if they picked up other Morphs on these planets, too. All of this was in English, so I thought maybe this generation of Morphs was born on earth.

I wondered how many rooms there were with

spaceships just like this one.

There were still many rooms on this gigantic spaceship that we hadn't seen. But it was just about time to get back to civilization, as we knew it. We left the ship and walked all around it. There were scores of smaller ships that I had seen working in the canyon near Maggie's ranch. Nick inspected the smallest of the ships and said the morph people would have to shrink themselves in order to fit inside. It was almost too much for us to think about.

We got on the handcar and headed back the way we had come. We closed up everything and pulled the rock back against the pocket door.

CHAPTER THIRTY-TWO

Nick and I sat at the table trying to decide what to do next. I suggested that we tell Sarah about the spaceships and the train stations "You're right, Joe, I know," Nick replied, "but let's think about it first. Our house will be swarming with dozens of military and civilian personnel. I think it would be difficult to live in that kind of disruption."

"Well, let's try to figure out a way to do this without losing our home," I said. "We need to figure out how the Morphs planned to get the spaceship out of the cave room. If we figure that out, no one needs to know about the entrance from our cave. Maybe Sarah can figure that part out. She has years of experience studying these ships."

Later that day, Nick called Sarah and told her about what we had found. She said she would be on the next plane west.

The following evening, Sarah showed up at the door. I let Nick and Sarah have some alone time before we got down to the business of spaceships.

Sarah was anxious to get started early the next morning. I had filled two backpacks with food, lots of food, flashlights, small tools and walkie-talkies.

I wasn't going with them into the cave, but I did drive them around to the part of the lake where the nine dragon subs were moored.

The two of them boarded one of the subs and soon disappeared underwater. Sarah called me on the walkie-talkie and told me they were fine and almost ready to disembark the sub and head to the spaceships.

"Enjoy yourselves," I said to her. "Call me when you are ready to be picked up."

After two days of not hearing from them, I began to get worried. I would give them till evening before I called to check up on them. Later that afternoon, Nick called to say they were on their way back, but not by sub. They were coming on the handcar through the train station would meet me at our private cave.

So fifteen minutes later, I slid down the slide to our pool and saw Nick and Sarah making their way through the third pocket.

"Wow, that looks like a lot of fun," Sarah smiled.

We sat at our glass table and they filled me in on their time on the spaceship.

Sarah said she would have to bring in a team of scientists to examine the new mother ship. "I don't want this to disrupt your entire lives, so let's not tell them about your cave. They can use the submarine entrance."

Sarah then said that she knew how the Morphs were going to get the spaceship out of the cave. "I'm not going to tell you right now—I'll show you in the morning."

The next day, we trekked back to the room with the new mother ship. We all climbed aboard and she told the two of us to hold on to the safety rails by the windows. She sat in the chair in front of the control panels. I wasn't sure what to think, but I was a bit nervous when she began pressing buttons and the ship revved to life. Blue and red lights shimmered all over the cave walls.

Sarah smiled devilishly at us and then pulled back on a large lever in front of her. The spacecraft lifted off the cave room floor and hovered about twenty feet up. As soon as it was high enough, the ship tilted toward the cave ceiling. We heard a loud rumbling sound, and the cave ceiling slowly opened. The morning sky came into view. Tree branches fell into the cave as the doors parted. It must have been many years since these overhead doors had been opened because the trees that had broken were very tall.

The ceiling doors completely opened and the ship eased its way out of the cave into the open sky. Once we had cleared the treetops, the ship leveled out and Sarah left the control panel. She smiled as I asked who was flying the ship.

"It flies itself," she said. "Not much different than the auto controls a commercial pilot sets."

I wanted to know why I wasn't floating.

"You aren't high enough, yet, but the Morphs have invented a machine that simulates gravity. It kicks on when it's needed," Sarah said.

I enjoyed watching the earth get smaller and smaller. Nick commented that the stars looked so much bigger and brighter.

Sarah said it was time to go back as she had never flown this far before. She had only done testing runs in the smaller spacecraft. Nick said he was beginning to feel strange and weightless. He held onto the rail and his feet began to rise above his head. I was having fun doing summersaults. I took off my watch and it floated, too. Nick, feeling brave, let go of the rails and grabbed the watch. Sarah laughed as she watched us try to wrestle each other in the air. She had deactivated the anti-gravity machine so we could experience weightlessness. She pressed a button and we both fell straight to the floor. Now it was time to go back. I hoped she was as good at getting back into the cave as she was getting out. She was successful and we got the cave all buttoned up. I wondered if the phone lines to the police station were lighting up with spaceship sightings!

We spent the rest of the day swimming and relaxing by the pool. Sarah said that she was going to have to call in her crew tomorrow. It would take them a few days to collect supplies and get here. We were okay with that as long as they didn't know about our cave.

A few days after Sarah's phone call to D.C., her crew began to arrive. Only her researchers came first. They needed to assess the area to see what needed priority attention. The one thing they didn't want was media attention. Their supplies were delivered in utility trucks so as not to be noticed. Personnel were dropped off in delivery trucks that were commonly seen at the carnival. It was all kept very quiet, which made us very thankful we had a good relationship with Sarah.

The team knew it would take months to search all of the rooms in the cave, let alone the amount of work it would take to study the aircraft.

Sarah could only stay for a week to get them started. She needed to return to her work at the Pentagon and domes.

We tried to settle into some type of routine while the crews were working in the caves. Nick missed Sarah, and I couldn't help but think about Maggie. No routine helped.

Weeks later, Sarah came to check on the progress of the work being done. She told us that a new hanger was being readied for the spaceships. Nick asked where it was being built.

"I can only tell you that it is somewhere in New Mexico," Sarah said. "But for now, it will stay right where it is. I will have a good excuse to come to visit more often."

Nick and Sarah went to a movie and I stayed home. I had a lot on my mind, so I went upstairs to think.

I figured that the Morph problem was probably

settled. What few were left would soon be caught or killed.

Steve was settled on base and was enjoying flight school. He and Becky loved being together whenever they could work it out; Nick was happily in love with Sarah. Things were slowly getting back to normal.

I assumed that Maggie, Gramps, and everyone missing on the ranch had been abducted and taken to Sagitar. I remembered what Cheryl said when we were sharing information at the underwater domes. I cannot imagine Maggie becoming anyone's pet. It sounded like there were other Morphs who were trying to exterminate the pets like we do rodents here. I hoped Maggie and Gramps wouldn't get caught in the crossfire between the two groups. I couldn't stop thinking about her, and I wondered if she was thinking of me.

At first, Zorko felt that he had won. He had Maggie and all of her family and ranch. He even had Schotzie. But this Joe character had become more and more necessary to have as part of the collection called Maggie. He continued reading the last entry in her journal. He was sure now, more than ever, that he had to have Joe.

I was slowly getting used to my new home. I wasn't happy, but I had become accustomed to my new way of life. Zorko had sold me to the High Commander with the promise of a promotion and a hefty profit. He said not only was he richer now, but he had thoroughly enjoyed the hunt for the perfect book set.

I was able to get a meeting with the HC and he promised me that my ranch would be moved next to Hitler's City. I would be in the country, but there were still places to meet people and do my ranching business.

I have been in Hitler's City now for several months. The HC comes by often to visit. He loves my ranch and has even bought some of my colts.

Sagitar is not very different from home in the way the cities are run. The HC is always trying to make improvements and build up the cities. He is even concerned that we small humans have a better, safer way to travel. He is working on building a better highway from our city to the next one.

Snicklesville is two miles away, which is a long distance because we are only six inches tall. We can only travel by foot or bicycle.

It's very dangerous to be out on the road. We are so small that Morph drivers don't always see us. Sometimes we get lost and end up in the desert and get eaten by the Snickles. Other times, big birds fly overhead and pluck us right off the road and use us as food for their babies. This new covered road will prevent these tragedies from happening. Having these improvements are some of the things that make our time here bearable. It keeps our minds off home.

When we were abducted and brought to this planet, we weren't all taken to the same town. Our families were split up and sold to other towns. Safer roads will make it easier to search for them.

The High Commander told me that, even though our planet is much bigger then earth, there are fewer people. Sagitar has what they call the Seven Year Rule. No one during the seventh year is allowed to have children. Not even us. The men are given a drug that makes them infertile for a year. That keeps our population down.

Sagitar has more resources than earth has. They have stronger metals on their planet. They found that when they added some of Sagitar's minerals to ours, they ended up with a metal that was both super strong and flexible.

The lands here are nutrient rich and make for wonderful gardens.

This planet has vast oceans full of fishlike beings. There are no toxins or poisons in the oceans so we are able to consume them without worry.

Sagitar's deserts are guarded by Snickles. They are like our gophers. They have very sharp teeth and live underground in colonies. We are a food source for them so we must stay out of the desert. They live mainly off the dead birds that land on the desert floor. The Snickles are about the only thing I'm afraid of here.

It was difficult, at first, to be thought of as a pet. They do take good care of us, though, and let us do whatever makes us happy.

I spend most of my days just like I did at home. I tend to the horses and breed them for the Morphs. They are a favorite of the wealthy Morphs. The buyers from Saudi Arabia work with me on the ranch. They help train the horses and generally keep the ranch running. Gramps seems to have a lot more energy, now, and he spends his day playing chess in the city park with the Germans.

Kitti and her kids stayed in the city. She married a nice German man and is happy. She likes the idea of living two thousand years.

The High Commander is considerate of the customs we had on earth. He has begun to understand what makes us think and act as we do.

Even though there are no holidays on Sagitar, the HC lets us celebrate whatever holidays we want. He will even bring us Thanksgiving turkeys and all the trimmings. He brings everyone Christmas presents. I think he likes the idea of a benevolent Santa. Last Christmas, I got a new watch and Gramps got new boots. Kitti and the kids got a special treat. They woke up Christmas morning to the sound of a dog barking. They ran downstairs to see Schotzie wagging her tail. They now feel like a complete family.

After work is done, I like to walk into the city. Even though it is evening, I like to walk along the city streets and look in the shop windows. It reminds me of home. The Morphs aren't greatly different from us; the women like fashion and the men like new gadgets. I end my evening walk with a peek in the barbershop window. I hold my breath and wait for the customer to turn around. I never stop hoping it will be Joe.

I usually sit outside at the café, remembering the coffees and ice cream Joe and I shared. My memories are all I have of him and are what keep me going. I order Sagitar's version of coffee and watch the children play in the street. Most evenings are peaceful. Sometimes we hear music performed at the Town Square; other evenings, couples just sit at the table and talk. But tonight, a man who looks like Hitler set up a platform. He shook his fist at the High Commander and warned him to beware. "Someday I will be the High Commander. Sagitar will be mine. I am ten thousand strong and growing."

I turn away and fade into my memories. My heart yearns for what could have been, what should have been. As I sip from the warm cup before me, I think of Joe and his strong arms around me. And I wonder if he still thinks of me.

Zorko still couldn't understand the emotions of these humans, but he did understand profit. He immediately put in his order for a transport.

It was late when Nick and Sarah got in from their date. A taxi was coming to pick her up because she had received a call from the Pentagon and had to catch an early flight back to D.C.

Sarah left in the wee hours of the morning and Nick couldn't sleep, so he had the coffee pot on very early. I woke up to the sound of talking. Steve had been given a week's leave. He was between classes and decided to come home to finish some projects in his room. The three of us enjoyed sitting around the table like old times.

We were catching Steve up on the latest events when we felt the warmth of the morning sun leave the kitchen. The room turned dark and an ominous quiet filled the air. We saw blue and red lights dancing on the kitchen walls and we knew they were coming for us.

ABOUT THE AUTHOR

Dennis Ray lives in Oregon with his wife, three dachshunds, and a parrot. Besides writing, he enjoys biking and fishing.

He has always had a desire to share his imagination with others. Since his retirement, he has written two books and is working on two more.

Cave Journals is his first publication; born out of his love for mysteries, science fiction, and mobster stories.

Made in the USA
Middletown, DE
07 May 2015